PRAISE FOR JA!

"What a wild ride! Moon Mask by James ... is the fastest moving and most riveting story I have read all year! Read it!" **Amazon.com reader review.**

"Think of Harrison Ford, Robert Langley, Angelina Joly, Flash Gordon and all the Boys own papers rolled into one and you get some idea of this rip-roaring tale of adventure." **Amazon.co.uk reader review.**

"James Rollins and Matthew Reilly have a serious rival!" **Amazon.co.uk reader review.**

"A cracking fast paced epic thriller in the vein of Matthew Reilly, James Rollins and Andy McDermott, and one of the best debut's of this genre I have read." **Goodreads reader review.**

They said Moon Mask by James Richardson is a "cross between Indiana Jones, James Bond, Leathal Weapon and a Die Hard film-script all in one." They were right. Super thrill ride interwoven with a great mystery with so many twists and turns I felt like I was on a roller Coaster!" **Goodreads reader review.**

Other adventures from the
WORLD OF MOON MASK

Requiem of a King: Animated text story

Dr King's Blog: The Progenitor Theory

Dr King's Blog: The Sarisariñama Expedition

The Xibalba Saga
- 1: The Xibalba Prophecy
- 2: The Xibalba Quest
- 3: The Xibalba Hunt
- 4: The Xibalba Curse
- 5: The Xibalba Secret

www.moonmask.net

THE XIBALBA PROPHECY

JAMES RICHARDSON

Copyright © 2022 James Richardson

This work is registered with The UK Copyright Service

The right of James Richardson to be identified as the Author of the Work has been asserted by him in accordance with the Copyright, Designs and Patents Act 1988.

All rights reserved. No part of this publication may be reproduced, stored in a retrieval system, or transmitted in any form or by any means, electronic, mechanical, photocopying, recording, or otherwise, without the prior permission of the copyright owner of this book.

All characters in this book are fictitious, and any resemblance to
actual persons living or dead is purely coincidental.

A CIP catalogue record for this book is available from the British Library.

First Edition Published in 2022

For Laura, my wife, my love, my friend.

For Xander and Kai, my boys, my life, my buddies

You are my world

PROLOGUE:

OFF THE COAST OF JAMAICA, 1725

THE stench of death engulfed the ominous black hulk of the slave ship.

The *L'aille Raptor* rolled on the ocean's swell, her rigging creaking in the breeze. A crystal-clear sky hung above, shimmering in the heat. Yet, despite the brilliance of the sunlight and its warmth upon Lieutenant Percival Lowe's skin, the deck seemed shrouded in a cold shadow.

The deck, masts, rigging and sails were dirty and in disarray, though clear of debris and undamaged. Yet not a single crewman, breathing or rotting, was to be seen. Even the gulls circled some distance away as though they also felt the menace the ship exuded.

Lowe had heard tales of these ghost ships; vessels found drifting at sea, their hulls intact, their gallies and holds full, yet the crew gone. His mind played through numerous fanciful scenarios, picturing sea monsters slithering up the deck, great tentacles dragging every last soul to a watery grave.

He sucked in another lungful of sea air, ordering his stomach to calm itself, embarrassed enough at having shown weakness in front of his men.

Following one of his boarding parties below deck moments ago, the sight that had greeted him was horrifying: two hundred black bodies, chained together, wrist to ankle, skin decaying, and lifeless eyes staring at the low ceiling. The stench of rotting flesh had slammed into Lowe's belly like a hammer blow, and he'd spun on the spot, racing back above decks just in time to throw up over the ship's side.

He glanced aft to ensure his ship, HMS *Swallow*, hadn't fallen into the same netherworld as the Raptor's crew. She remained at station keeping and, beyond her, in the distance, lay the faint outline of Jamaica's golden coast.

Satisfied that the rest of his breakfast would not be floating on the Caribbean swell, he wiped a handkerchief over his lips and chin, glancing at Gil.

"They were all slaves," he said, bile burning his throat. "But where is the crew?"

"Looks like the slaves all starved to death, sir," Gil replied, his wild mane of grey hair dancing on the breeze. Three decades Lowe's senior, by age rather than rank, his pale eyes seemed unfazed by what they had seen. "We found one alive, though."

"Alive?" Lowe repeated, shocked.

"Don't ask me how the devil he's alive, sir, but alive he is."

Lowe nodded. He wouldn't put it beyond these lesser races to resort to cannibalism to survive.

"But the crew?" Lowe asked again. "What happened to the crew?"

A call from astern halted Gil's tongue, catching their attention.

"We've found them, sir," Jenkins ran towards him, his boyish face ashen.

Lowe's heart thudded. "And?" he snapped. "Are they alive?"

Jenkins stared at him for long moments, eyes wide. "You better take a look, sir."

Lowe masked his reluctance and followed the young man below decks to the crew barracks. The door was closed, but the stench of decay already wafted into his nostrils. He demanded his stomach to be stronger this time.

"It was bolted shut," another crewman explained, standing in front of the heavy wooden door.

"From the outside," Jenkins added.

"Somebody locked them in?" Lowe asked.

"Aye . . . thank the lord," Jenkin's said. Lowe glowered at the boy, but Jenkins' companion cut in before he could admonish the lad.

"Are you ready, sir?"

Lowe hesitated, his rational mind screaming at him not to open the door, confident he didn't want to see what was behind it.

"Sir?" Gil prompted, highlighting his misgivings.

"Yes, yes!" Lowe snarled, masking his fear with anger. "Get on with it."

The door swung open.

Lowe gasped.

The image of the starved slaves was nothing compared to the horror that confronted him now.

The ship's cargo looked like dead humans, albeit savage Africans. The crew, however, looked as though they were the monsters that had sealed their own fate.

Hideous whelps and blisters covered their bodies. Many had burst and seeped over the deck before drying into a sticky residue. Human hair, large tufts which had fallen from scalps before the natural decomposition of death had begun, stuck to the grotesque glue. The stinking remains were twisted and gnarled as though they had died in agony.

Dead eyes stared at him as he staggered back out of the room. The dregs of his breakfast raced up his throat, but he swallowed it, retaining a modicum of pride.

"It's a plague ship," Gil exclaimed, making the sign of the cross with his hands. "The crew must have succumbed. Then, with no one to feed them, the slaves starved."

Before anyone could utter another word, a strange squelching noise came from behind them, followed by Jenkins' startled cry. The party of men spun to see the young man's body stiffen, eyes wide with confusion, shock, and then terror. He looked down his torso at the bloodied blade erupting from his belly.

Lowe watched that blade slide back through the sailor's body, allowing it to crumple to the deck and revealing, behind it, the most terrifying thing he'd ever seen.

The attacker's body was almost naked, mere rags clinging to a dirty, blood-smeared torso. Lowe could see the same agonising blisters as the rest of the dead crew, oozing and weeping putrid puss like a damaged tree exuded sap.

Lowe could not tell whether the blisters covered the monster's face. A brightly coloured mask glared back at him instead of a human visage.

Hung on the wall of a stately home, it might have been a thing of beauty. Thousands of tiny red, green, yellow and blue beads swirled around the cheeks and eyes. A reddish-gold coloured sheet of hammered metal encompassed the forehead, etched with geometric patterns. Dots of precious stones formed an elaborate design around the mouth like a tattoo.

The thing itself possessed an almost benevolent persona, rounded and gentle. But the bloodshot orbs glowering through the mask's eyes were wild and mad.

Lowe gasped, realising that the man in the mask was not an escaped Negro, but one of the ship's officers. He swung his bloodied sword up and unleashed a terrifying war cry.

"Savage mumbo-jumbo!"

Jenkins' murderer hurled himself at Lowe and his two remaining men.

They staggered backwards, Gil throwing himself between his lieutenant and their attacker, letting out a wail as the attacker cleaved a wad of flesh and muscle from his arm. In the commotion, Lowe fell backwards, landing on top of one of the hideous corpses. He cried out in terror and promptly threw up the last of his coveted breakfast.

The man in the mask thrust his sword at Lowe's last remaining man, sinking it up to the hilt in his chest before wrenching it back out with a manic cry.

The monstrous man turned towards the sprawled naval officer as he backpedalled away, splattered with fresh gore, sliding through the foul, sticky residue on the deck. His body quaked with terror, his limbs betraying him. The man in the mask leapt towards him, moving like an animal rather than a human. He grasped the sword between both hands, ready to plunge it into the lieutenant's heart.

Lowe acted on instinct, wrenching his pistol from its holster and firing at the beast, the ball striking the man mid-air.

He hit the deck with a thud.

There, you bastard, he thought. *Go back to whatever hell you climbed out of.*

Trembling, Lowe watched the figure. It was motionless for a time, but then he heard the wretched man's rasping breath. Faint at first, but getting louder, stronger.

The masked face turned to glare at him, the raging fire in his eyes now twisting into cold fury. The figure rose, ignorant of the blood pouring from the bullet wound to his shoulder, soaking what rags remained on him.

Not just any rags, Lowe realised with horror. The tattered clothes had once been smart and expensive, a white cotton shirt, damask waistcoat and a scarlet scarf suggesting a man of wealth and prestige ... the captain of one of Britain's most profitable slave enterprises.

"Captain Pryce?" Lowe gasped, remembering the *L'aille Raptor's* master's name from his own captain's report before being sent to board the ship. He kept his gun arm straight but could not halt its shaking. "What ... what happened?"

Pryce took one slow, menacing step toward him after another. Lowe's eyes watched a bead of blood run down the blade's edge and splash onto the deck.

"Savage mumbo-jumbo," Pryce croaked.

"You ... your crew ... you locked them down here ..."

"Savage mumbo-jumbo," Pryce muttered again.

"We are here to help, Captain. My ship ... is just astern-"

"Savage mumbo-jumbo," the man in the mask repeated, stopping by Lowe's feet and raising his sword. Lowe closed his eyes and pulled his pistol's trigger but, as he had known, nothing happened, his single shot already fired and wasted.

"Please . . . remove the mask, Captain," he sobbed.

"Savage," Pryce snarled, "mumbo-jumbo!"

Lowe screamed as the sword plunged towards his chest-

Another figure burst from the shadows just before the tip pierced his skin.

One-handed, Gil swung an enormous block of wood at Pryce's head, knocking him away from Lowe. If not for the protection of the mask, the blow would have cleaved Pryce's skull. Instead, he staggered, dropping to his hands and knees on the deck, the mask falling from his face.

A high-pitched yelp escaped Lowe's throat.

Some considered Captain Edward Pryce a monster, Lowe knew. His ruthless efficiency and treatment of his cargo ensured the best prices at auction. But the captain's metamorphosis into such a beast, Lowe realised, was now complete.

However monstrous in spirit he had once been, Pryce was certainly human no more. Most of his flesh had rotted away. What remained was puckered, scarred and blistered, stretched taut over an almost hairless scalp. His nose had crumbled away, and his lip-less mouth's raw, red muscles drew back into a cry of anguish.

Lowe thought the cry was one of embarrassment, humiliation at his appearance. But then he realised that Pryce had forgotten about Gil and himself and that his despair was at having lost the mask.

He hurled himself at it, gathering it into his arms like a lost lover, observing the damage Gil had inflicted, the dent, the missing beads. He whimpered, nursing the mask like an infant.

"Savage mumbo-jumbo," he whispered, stroking the African idol, repeating his mantra while rocking back and forth.

Gil raised his improvised weapon, ready to swing it down and end the miserable creature's life. But Lowe jumped to his feet and halted his man's actions. He saw the old sea dog grapple with his anger and, for a moment, thought he might disobey him. Instead, he dropped the plank of wood.

Lowe turned his pitying attention back to the broken, disfigured form of Edward Pryce as he cradled the mask, rocking and weeping.

"Savage mumbo-jumbo," he whimpered, "savage mumbo-jumbo, savage mumbo-jumbo . . ."

BALTIMORE
MARYLAND, USA

PRESENT DAY

"**BUT** it doesn't make any goddamn sense!"

The woman's voice was so loud and angry that it drifted through the closed door. "One of my team recognised him – he's a radiologist." There was a pause, presumably while the voice on the other end of the woman's phone replied.

"That's ridiculous," Doctor Lorna Burke's voice continued. "I know the patient's symptoms suggest radiation poisoning, but I've checked half a dozen times – there is no evidence of radiological material in or on her. She's suffering from a tropical disease, and I need to be in her room treating her, not waiting outside while some dinosaur who retired almost thirty years ago comes up with some phoney diagnosis to appease his CIA overlords."

Dinosaur? Emmett Braun repeated in his head, allowing a silent chuckle to warm the icy dread he felt slowly permeating his body. Looking down at his shriveled hands, he supposed *dinosaur* was a fair enough assessment.

He turned his attention back to the girl on the bed. The CIA agents had stripped any indication of her name, previous medical history or recent background from her file. She was simply Patient JH28791.

He understood Doctor Burke's frustration, of course. The patient's symptoms - nausea, vomiting, diarrhoea and high fever, followed by skin ulceration, abnormal fatty growth, bruising, hair loss and unconsciousness – suggested acute radiation exposure. Yet neither her blood work nor several varieties of detectors had identified radiation in her system.

While he understood the doctor's frustration, he knew that arguing with her superiors was useless. Emmett's babysitters would have taken this to the highest level possible, probably batting around words like 'national security' to get their way. The hospital bosses wouldn't go against the wishes of the CIA.

Emmett returned to the task at hand by tuning out of Burke's argument and trying to ignore the watchful gaze of Agents Jones and Tomkins. He cast his mind back through all the patients he had treated through his decades-long career in private health care and the navy.

How many of you did I fail? He wondered. From Hiroshima and Nagasaki to Chernobyl and Fukushima, he'd been involved in almost every major radioactive accident since the splitting of the atom. His work to develop more effective treatments for acute radiation sickness earned him a Nobel Prize. His so-called 'selfless' act to come out of retirement and help those endangered by Fukushima's meltdown saw his photo on the cover of Time magazine.

Yet, for all the good he had done, the lives he had saved, there were so many more he had failed. None more so than the poor wretches he turned his memory back to now.

At least she seems peaceful, he thought, glancing again at Patient JH28791. Even though the twitches of the woman's eyes behind her lids and the erratic activity on the EEG screen suggested otherwise, he knew her coma saved her from far worse. The screaming, the shouting, the blood-

"Doctor," a man's voice snapped him back to

the moment. He realised he'd shut his eyes, allowing the memory, the nightmare, to wash over him.

"Sorry," he stammered. He saw the loathing in Agent Jones' eyes. He imagined he and his partner had joined the CIA to see some action, not to babysit a dithering old man who seemed to have actually fallen asleep on the job.

Jones' face suggested he had called his name several times before getting through to him. Now, the flash of annoyance was replaced by pity.

Don't pity me, Emmett thought, placing a hand on the sleeping girl's arm, hoping she felt his presence and took some comfort from it. *Pity her.*

The door flung open before he could say anything further. Doctor Burke marched in, her face set hard, her eyes angry. Her silver-streaked black hair was tied into a tight ponytail, and she pulled her white coat tighter around herself, as though raising a shield.

"I don't give a damn who you people are," she started, jabbing her phone at Jones and Tomkins. "Or if my boss tells me to stand down. That's my patient lying there, and the only way I'm leaving her side is if you carry me out screaming and yelling."

Jones exchanged a glance with Tomkins, then shrugged. "Done," he said. The shock on Burke's face told Emmett the agents had called her bluff. Yet she stood firm, glaring past them at him.

"That won't be necessary," Emmett cut in before the situation escalated.

Jones and Tomkins turned to him askance. "Are you saying it's-"

"It's confirmed," Emmett said. The words caught in his throat and made his stomach churn. He couldn't believe it. He didn't want to believe it. But there was no denying the truth.

He had been out fishing, enjoying the gentle swell rocking his little blue boat back and forth, when the CIA agents had turned up at his house yesterday afternoon. He never went far, and, from his canvas chair on the deck, with his feet up on his chiller box and a bottle of Bud in his hand, he could see his house on the shore. Gulls circled above, waiting for the frenzy that his catch would instil in them.

Then his radio had hissed to life. It was Martha, his wife. Emmett had noted the anxiety in her voice immediately.

The agents gave all the usual crap about national security. Still, Martha had reminded them that he was ninety-three years old and had retired from the navy decades ago. He had done his duty. He had gone beyond it.

Then Jones had muscled into the radio call, relaying a cryptic message that meant nothing to him but everything to Emmett.

"The Phoenix has arisen."

The devil's icy finger had seemed to glide down his spine, the words chilling him to the core.

It can't be, he'd thought. Hoped. Prayed.

Indeed, even the devil would not dare involve himself in such monstrous business.

Hours later, a private jet landed him and his babysitters at BWI airport. Dawn had yet to break above the Baltimore skyline, but Jones and Tomkins offered no respite for their elderly companion, whisking him straight to John Hopkins hospital.

Now, Jones whipped out his cell phone. The call was answered instantly, and, without needing to identify himself, the CIA agent relayed his two-worded report to his superior.

"It's confirmed."

"What?" Burke demanded, her glare accusing. "What have you confirmed?"

You don't want to know, my dear, Emmett silently replied. Tomkins pushed the woman back. If Emmett had been a few decades younger, he would have protested the violence. But his mind still reeled from his diagnosis, and he turned back to the chaotic lines on the patient's EEG reading.

I may have confirmed the cause of her symptoms, he thought, *but I'm not qualified to determine their ramifications. But I know of someone who is.*

His heartrate increased as he glanced back at the commotion as Tomkins forced Doctor Burke out the room, Jones finishing his call and coming to his aid.

Then, before losing his nerve, he pulled his smartphone from his pants pocket, hit the camera shortcut on the side, and quickly took a shot of the EEG readout. Then he pocketed the device and scribbled on the patient's notes. He stashed them back into the holder at the foot of her bed just as Tomkins slammed the door shut behind Burke.

Jones turned to him. Emmett saw a flash of suspicion in the agent's eyes and did his best to look innocent. Too innocent, perhaps. He averted his gaze to the patient. "So, what happens now?" he asked.

Jones paused for a second longer, then held out a key fob. "Your job's done. There's a rental car in the parking lot. Hotel and flight details in the glove box." He spoke robotically, as though reciting from a script. Emmett, however, paid little attention to his words, too lost in the implications of what he'd just seen.

"Thank you for your service, Doctor," Jones finished, the platitude an afterthought. The next few minutes passed in a blur for Emmett. He didn't argue his dismissal, merely left the hospital room, throwing a final glance at the poor woman on the bed. He wound his way through the corridors into the parking lot, using the license plate number on the key fob to identify his rental car.

It wasn't until he slammed the door shut that he let out a deep breath and sagged into the driver's seat. He rubbed his eyes with the ball of each hand as though the motion could erase the image of men and women writhing in agony from them.

Not again, he thought. *Not again.*

Hands shaking, he plucked his cell phone from his pocket, resisting the urge to call Martha. Instead, he pulled up the illicit photo he had taken inside the patient's room.

Trying to remember his granddaughter's instructions on operating the smartphone, he opened the web browser. Joy could have done it in no time, he knew. Hell, even Martha was faster than him. But eventually, he conducted a search through the staff profiles of Cornell University, found the email address he was looking for and attached the photo.

He typed a simple message: *did they do it?*

His finger hovered over the *send* button.

He knew he'd spend the rest of his life behind bars if they found out.

They'll brand me a traitor. Maybe even an Enemy of the State. They won't just let a secret like this get out.

He moved his finger to hit *cancel* just as movement caught his eye in the rear-view mirror. Two men approached the rear of his car. Their heads were down, hoods up, their clothes scruffy. *Drop-outs,* he realised, *a couple of lowlifes.*

But then he noticed something else: their shoes were black, polished, matching. And then it hit him.

"Of course," he whispered.

The photo didn't matter. The email didn't matter. He should have known they wouldn't allow him to live now that his task was complete.

Heart hammering the inside of his ribcage, he hit *send.* Then he fumbled with the key fob, taking too long to realise it wasn't a traditional key but some newfangled electronic fob. The engine finally purred to life.

He glanced in the mirror again. This time he recognised the face of one of the hooded men: Agent Jones.

He slammed the car into drive and stomped on the gas, squealing away as two shots rang out. Glass shattered, exploding into the vehicle. But the inevitable impact of bullets slamming into his back never came.

Wind whistled inside as he hauled the steering wheel around to the left. The Ford Mercury sedan slewed across the road in response. A cacophony of horns blared in his wake as he cut across Orleans Street and barrelled down Hillen towards the interstate.

He might have believed the cover story himself. Baltimore was a big city, after all. Muggings and murders occurred all the time. If not for the agents' sloppy error, forgetting to change their footwear, he'd probably be dead now.

He snapped out of his lapse in concentration to avoid slamming into a speeding truck. The large vehicle's lights flashed, and its horn echoed as he shot through an underpass and then circled around, speeding up as he tore onto the interstate. In his rear-view mirror, he saw the flash of a black SUV thundering towards him, dashing between lanes to close the gap.

Jones and Tomkins.

He snatched his attention back to the front, whipping around a bus.

Interstate 83 was busy, the rush hour traffic whirring around him. His hands trembled as they clutched the steering wheel. Dazed, he struggled to control the surge of adrenalin pumping through his body. His mind sorted through his memories, trying to think of anyone who could help him.

"Shit!" Emmett cursed, pounding the brakes to avoid smashing into the back of a brown Station Wagon, plodding along slowly in the fast lane.

He could picture Martha's frown, scolding him

for the use of foul language. He felt a swell of despair at the thought of never seeing her again.

"Concentrate!" he ordered himself.

Martha would be the first to tell him that it was never too late, that there was always a chance.

With renewed determination, he hammered the rental's horn and flashed his lights, ordering the Station Wagon out of the way. Then he floored the gas again, squeezing through the narrow gap between the brown car and the centre of the road, ignoring the other driver's raised middle finger.

Behind him, the black SUV pushed in front of the bus that Emmett had already passed. It hauled between two other angry drivers to plant itself in the fast lane directly behind Emmett.

He glanced in his mirror as the assassins closed the gap. Their higher-powered vehicle raced towards him just as the brown Station Wagon clipped his aft quarters. Its driver was more invested in flicking him the birdy than checking his mirrors. He had swerved back into the fast lane to avoid a large orange and black Home Depot truck powering up the middle one.

It was only a glancing blow but, pushing one hundred miles an hour, Emmett lost control. The steering wheel spun on its own accord. He felt the vehicle slew out, its front end intersecting the middle lane.

The Station Wagon driver screamed as he rammed into Emmet's broadside.

The sedan flipped over, and Emmett heard the crunch of metal and the screech of rubber above his scream as the car rolled over once, twice, three times. His world shrank as the metal of the vehicle compressed on him. His head smashed the windscreen, the steering wheel, the roof, the chair, and the erupting airbags. He realised he hadn't fastened his safety belt and rolled around inside the crushed wreck.

But no safety belt or airbag could have saved him from the Home Depot truck.

Even as its driver fought with the brakes, its twenty-foot-long trailer swung from side to side. It took out half a dozen other vehicles before slamming into the crumpled sedan.

The impact wrenched the smaller vehicle into two separate pieces. They spun away from each other, rolling and twisting until, at last, they came to a stop.

BEHIND the carnage, Agent Jones skidded the black SUV to a halt while hundreds of other vehicles did the same for miles behind. Within moments, Interstate 83 was gridlocked. Car horns echoed, and angry voices shouted out, indignant about the sudden halt to their journeys home.

"Did you see that?" Tomkins asked.

Jones glanced at his subordinate and noticed that the younger man's face had lost its colour as he stared ahead. About a dozen vehicles were caught up with Emmett Braun's death, the wrecked hulks of cars, trucks and buses belching smoke into the sunset.

"Of course I saw it," he snapped. He clambered out of the SUV and headed towards the remains of Braun's rental car. Tomkins had the good sense to follow.

Emergency sirens already wailed as the first responders battled through the gridlock to the crash site. People from the first rows of cars to escape the carnage rushed to help the survivors.

"Well, I don't think we're gonna get our rental deposit back on that," Tomkins tried to joke.

Jones ignored him and focussed on the charred and bloodied figure crushed within the folds of metal that had once been the sedan. Then he pulled his cell phone out and called the pre-programmed number.

"It's done," he said.

LOCATION: UNKNOWN

THE man in the yellow tie rubbed the bridge

of his nose, trying to alleviate the pain that throbbed behind his eyes. It had started the moment he'd been briefed on the situation. It only got worse as he immersed himself in the details surrounding Patient JH28791.

An archaeologist working on the United Nations Educational, Scientific and Cultural Organisation-funded 'Sarisariñama Expedition,' she had been airlifted from the remote site in Venezuela after falling ill.

The emergency evacuation was the only point of excitement in what had proven to be an overrated, over-funded mess of competing personalities and archaeological theories. After six months, the expedition had amounted to nothing.

It had started promisingly enough, an applaudable response to the accidental discovery of ancient ruins. Kira Sharpe, a so-called billionaire playgirl, had illegally base-jumped into an enormous sinkhole on the summit of Sarisariñama, one of Venezuela's famous table mountains. The hole's thick foliage had caught her chute, swinging her into the vegetation-encrusted wall. But there, totally unexpected, hidden for hundreds of years by the thick vines and lush tropical vegetation, was a doorway hewn into the rock. That doorway led to a series of passageways tunnelling into the two-hundred square mile summit, sparking huge academic debate over their origins.

Lauded as the archaeological find of the century, UNESCO had organised the expedition. Numerous commercial sponsors, notably Sharpe Enterprises, provided most of the funding. They promised a real-time adventure on the scale of an Indiana Jones movie, presented to the world through buzzing social media updates, blogs and live video streaming. But, after six months, the expedition had unearthed nothing: no ancient artefacts, no human remains, not even a room or chamber. There was nothing at Sarisariñama except mile after mile of identical tunnels.

But there *was* something else there, the man in the yellow tie knew.

As if on cue, a melodic chime announced the arrival of an email; it might as well have been an apocalyptic dong.

The man in the yellow tie opened his inbox, glancing past the usual bureaucratic clutter to focus on the latest receipt.

Double-clicking the attachment, an encrypted file unspooled, displaying a medical report for Patient JH28791. It confirmed everything the man in the yellow tie needed to know: that, over eight thousand feet above sea level, defended by almost vertical cliffs on all sides, hundreds of miles from the nearest road and accessible only by helicopter, Sarisariñama, one of the most isolated places on the planet, harboured a secret.

A terrifying secret.

Pulling his phone from his breast pocket, he dialled a number from memory. He listened to the soft squeals of the signal running through an encryption program. When it connected, a gruff voice answered.

"Yes?"

The man in the yellow tie cut straight to the point. "It's confirmed." He glanced at Patient JH28791's plump but pretty face on the medical report and wondered how she had got herself caught up in all of this.

Then he thought about the rest of the UN expedition. It was a multi-disciplined team of archaeologists, anthropologists, biologists, botanists, zoologists, and entomologists. A group of local workers, cooks and porters supported them, and an Adventure Channel film crew documented the mission.

Now, the entire expedition was in his way.

He took a breath, then issued a simple order: "proceed."

2:

THE LABYRINTH, SARISARIÑAMA TEPUI, VENEZUELA

BENJAMIN King crashed through the ancient wall, dust pluming around him. His head smashed the ground, his yellow hard hat taking the brunt of the impact, even as he rolled down the steep incline, leaving it behind. Jagged stone blocks tumbled after him, clattering down the slope to slam into his ribcage.

"Ben!" Sid screamed.

"Get back!" Nadia shouted as the destruction King had wrought continued.

Unlike the refined engineering precision of the

rest of the subterranean tunnels, the wall that the three archaeologists had stumbled upon seemed crude, little more than a barrier of rocks and stones pasted together with blobs of grey mortar.

Karen's team had investigated this part of the Labyrinth before her medical evacuation two days ago. They had determined the poorly constructed barrier to be nothing more than another dead-end.

The jig-saw puzzle walls of the rest of the tunnel system, reminiscent of the Incan Polygonal Masonry found throughout the distant Andes, were polished smooth. The blocks sat so snuggly together that few roots from Sarisariñama's jungle-choked summit had broken through. Indeed, Andean examples of the construction technique were cut so precisely that they formed structures strong enough to withstand earthquakes that would topple modern buildings.

Yet, the blocks the three archaeologists had found here were rough. Their unfinished surfaces and ill-fitting shapes allowed thick roots to snake down, cocooning the stone face in a spiderweb-like crust of vegetation.

"It's a partition," King had realised, pushing against the structure, feeling the blocks shift under his weight, unsupported on the far side. "Added after the tunnels' original construction."

That was the moment the wall had given out. Unable to regain his footing, he had smashed through it, triggering a domino effect as block after block tumbled and fell.

Now, all King could do was huddle into the foetal position and clamp his eyes shut until the rumble of falling rock eased.

"Ben?" Sid called again.

"I'm okay," he coughed, uncertain he was telling the truth. He opened an eye, squinting into the darkness of the Labyrinth, his breath pluming around him in rapid puffs of vapour.

The term 'Labyrinth' was an unofficial designation for the Sarisariñama Ruins. It was a sprawling array of tunnels twisting and undulating through the table mountain, often running into dead-ends, sometimes looping around to re-join other branches.

The passageways went nowhere. They achieved nothing beyond channelling rainwater runoff from the surface. But even that seemed to have no place to go, merely sluicing around the bends like some Indiana Jones-themed waterpark.

King had suggested that the ancient facility was a water management system. However, Professor McKinney and her UNESCO funders were uncomfortable with that notion. It was embarrassing to admit they had mounted a multi-million-dollar, high-profile, public-facing expedition to investigate what amounted to an ancient sewer.

Not that the foul-tempered Scottish Lara Croft-wannabe ever entertains my theories anyway, King thought.

She could have utilised the expertise of one of the co-developers of the Universal Motif Language to interpret the single piece of epigraphic evidence found at Sarisariñama. Instead, she had him wandering the corridors, recording measurements and scribbling down observations that any first-year undergrad student could have completed.

"Ben?" Sid called, her torch beam zipping around the corridor he had fallen into, struggling to find him. "Where are you?"

"Here," he said, wincing as he scrambled upright. Chunks of ancient masonry rolled off him, but he was unharmed other than a few bruises.

"I can't see you."

"I'm here," he shouted, coughing to clear his throat. He couldn't see his hard hat or its attached torch. He guessed it lay buried under the rubble.

"This is precisely why it is a requirement for all expedition personnel to wear hi-vis jackets while in the tunnels," Nadia's clipped, Russian accent highlighted.

King rolled his eyes just as Sid's torch beam

locked onto them, blinding him. "Whoa," he snapped, shielding his face.

"Sorry." The light shifted away-

"Shit!" King yelped, bounding to his feet and back-peddling away, any ache and pain forgotten in his terror.

As his girlfriend's torch beam had swung away from him for a fraction of a second, he saw a face glaring at him from the darkness.

The ghost stories he had scoffed at exploded in the front of his mind.

Other expedition members reported seeing movement in the empty tunnels. They had heard strange sounds, like the rasping breath of a dying man, whispering from the darkness. Tools and equipment had vanished, only to be found far from where they had been used last.

"I don't believe in ghost stories," he had scoffed at each report. He put the paranormal scenarios down to the overactive imagination of men and women working underground for hours.

But, as a cold hand clutched his heart, he knew there was no explanation for what he had seen.

It could not be a fellow teammate. The wall he had accidentally demolished was the western-most point of the Labyrinth yet investigated, the other teams far away. Nor was what he saw a mere shadow;

the vision was etched in his minds-eye, a vivid, white face glaring at him, teeth bared as though a rabid animal, ready to strike.

I don't believe in ghost stories!

"Ben?" Sid called from the other side of the wall, her torch beam whipping around, disorienting him.

He couldn't have rolled further than two metres from the partition, yet it felt like an acre, the darkness pressing onto him. He kept his eyes fixed on the point where he had seen the apparition, but it felt as though the monster was all around him, as though a thousand pairs of invisible eyes were watching him.

"Ben, what's happening?" Nadia demanded, pushing past Sid to clamber over the demolished wall.

"No!" King barked. "Get back, get back!"

Something brushed his shoulder, and he spun around.

Shit!

Another face was there, inches from his, dancing in the panicked torch beams of his companions, leering at him with malevolence.

"There's something in here!" he shouted, pulling himself free of his captor. He scrambled towards the wall like a swimmer thrashing for the shore, knowing a shark hunted from below.

An explosion of light overloaded his retinas,

outlining the lithe silhouette of the Russian woman. Nadia stood on top of the half-demolished wall. She cracked a light stick with a single smack against her thigh, the chemicals mixing to illuminate their surroundings for the first time in thousands of years.

She threw it over King's head, his eyes drawn behind it as it revealed his monstrous hunters in all their horrific glory.

His step faltered; he sagged to the ground in front of the wall. The overdose of adrenaline made his heart jackhammer against his ribcage. A wave of embarrassment washed over him, amplified by the patronising arch of Nadia's right eyebrow and the merest hint of a grin on her usually stoic face.

"I thought you didn't believe in ghost stories," she pointed out. There was something vaguely supernatural about the silent agility she demonstrated as she leapt from the wall and into the corridor. The high visibility strips of her yellow safety vest, obediently donned on her entrance into the Labyrinth, drove home King's indignation.

"Ben," Sid gasped, scrambling over the wall and dropping next to him. With the light stick illuminating the tunnel, her helmet-mounted torch was less painful but still stabbed at his eyes. "Are you okay?"

She scanned his face for signs of injury, noting

a trickle of blood snaking down his black skin. The circular scar, seared into the centre of his forehead as a child, burned with embarrassment. It was a 'tell' she had picked up on years ago.

Sid turned her attention to the rest of his body. While King, to McKinney and her safety advisors' chagrin, refused to wear a hi-vis vest, he was rarely seen without his battered leather waistcoat.

It had been a gift from his dad when he had gone on his first voluntary archaeological dig, fifteen years old and full of enthusiasm. It was riddled with waterproof pockets, inside and out, and contained everything that King insisted he needed. Sid often joked that the ugly thing was like Mary Poppins' handbag, forever spewing out whatever he needed in any situation. Yet, while she detested the thing, she couldn't deny that the heavy leather had saved him from more significant injury. It had protected him like a layer of armour from the large stones that had rolled after him.

"I'm fine," he replied, waving her away. His eyes stared past her, down the length of the tunnel, and, as Sid followed his gaze, she gasped.

Row after row of human skulls lined the tunnel on either side, shimmering in the red glow of Nadia's light-stick, stretching into the gloom beyond. Held in place by more blobs of mortar, like the partition wall, they rose from the ground to the ceiling.

Pushed from above, several blocks of the vaulted roof had succumbed to the power of the jungle's root system, crashing to the stone floor. Fibrous tendrils coiled over the macabre scene, like the sinuous embrace of a dark leviathan coveting its feast.

"What is this place," Sid whispered. While the Mumbai-born woman struggled with the constant frigidity of the Labyrinth, it wasn't the temperature that caused her to pull her padded, hi-vis coat tighter.

"It appears to be a catacomb," Nadia said.

"Yeah," King agreed, staggering to his feet. Embarrassment at his panicked reaction to the torch-lit skull evaporated under his excitement. "But it's not part of the original structure. Look how much narrower this corridor is than the rest of the Labyrinth."

Sid followed him away from the partition wall but glanced back the way they had come. Sure enough, the tunnel leading to the partition was at least four-feet wider than the skull-lined corridor.

"It's like the most recent tenants added a creepy veneer to the original walls," she agreed. "Then sealed it up."

"There are hundreds of them," King said, winding down the corridor. He peered at row upon row of long-dead faces, piled three-deep against the original walls.

"Approximately four thousand, eight hundred individual specimens, based on the number of skulls alone, and within the ten-metre stretch of the tunnel we can see."

King and Sid stared at Nadia in bewilderment.

"Give or take . . ?" Sid teased, eliciting a flash of irritation behind the Russian's blue eyes.

Osteoarchaeology was Nadia Yashina's third degree and second PhD, a far cry from her original field of theoretical quantum physics or even applied-medicine. Her genius-level IQ, spotted and nurtured at an early age, had earned her recognition as one of the most intelligent people in the world.

She wasn't someone used to defending her conclusions.

Ignoring Sid's attempt at humour, Nadia glowered at both her companions. "We must report this discovery to Professor McKinney."

King felt as though the Russian had just slapped him around the face. "What? We've not even checked this passageway out yet."

"Nadia's right, Ben," Sid added. "We've got to report in."

"But who knows what else might be down here?" he argued.

"Precisely," Sid pressed, wiping dust off her mocha skin. Although raised in Britain, excitement often betrayed her accent, inherited from her father, rather than any time spent in India. "No one knows what's down here. More to the point, no one knows *we're* here. If something happens to us, they won't know to look for us in a hidden passageway: it's hidden, you see, that's kinda the point."

"The procedure is to report any unmapped passages before proceeding," Nadia added.

"And let McKinney and her brown-nosers find whatever's down here and take the credit? No way! After six months, this is the first thing anyone on this expedition has found other than miles of identical tunnels."

"The biological survey identified an undocumented butterfly species," Nadia argued.

King frowned, shaking his head. "This is our discovery," he concluded. "The three of us. Make your report if you want, but I'm taking a better look around."

He headed off again, this time with the tell-tale gait of a man who had made up his mind. Sid rolled her eyes and glanced at Nadia. "Why can't he ever be that passionate about me?" Then she headed after him. A heartbeat later, and without saying a word, Nadia fell into step too.

Despite the Russian's desire to follow procedure, King could tell that somewhere under her cold exterior, she was as excited as he was.

"Poor Karen," Sid said, feeling a twinge of guilt at having made this discovery in the excavation section that the sick woman's team had spent months exploring. "Can you believe she missed out on this find?"

King plucked the light stick from the floor and held it out before him as he proceeded down the skull-lined tunnel. Shadows danced and shifted, unsettling him but, already embarrassed, he pushed through his misgivings.

The incline of the floor grew steeper as they progressed and followed the passage around a sharp bend, almost doubling back under their path. Skulls continued to line the walls as far as they could see through the gloom, several of them smashed by blocks that had fallen from the ceiling, dropping a curtain of roots across their path. Pushing through it, the air grew even colder than the rest of the Labyrinth and an acrid stench, which King had noticed earlier, became more intense.

"What's that smell?" Sid asked, scrunching her nose in disgust while running her torch over the rack of skulls to her left. A whole section of the ceiling, at least two metres across, had collapsed, smashing dozens of craniums.

"Careful," King warned as she approached the damage.

"The structural integrity of the Labyrinth has, thus far, been uncompromised," Nadia reminded them.

As testimony to the Labyrinth Builders' architectural capabilities, out of the many miles of tunnels mapped so far, only one had succumbed to the astounding weight of the mountain above it.

"It seems the modifications made to this section have weakened the overall structure," Nadia added.

"I'm being careful," Sid said, knowing Nadia's observations were her way of transmitting concern. Nevertheless, she glanced at the tumble of earth spilt from above as she knelt next to a section of the smashed wall. One skull lay upturned on the floor, her torch beam glinting off the surface of water contained within. Noting an iridescent film, however, she sniffed it.

"Oil," she reported, identifying the source of the smell. But, glancing back up at King, she realised that his attention was elsewhere.

"Look at that," he whispered, eyes wide.

Sid moved to his side, wrapping a hand around his muscled forearm. "What?" she asked but cut herself off as she followed his gaze.

The bend in the tunnel straightened into a long avenue, still decorated by skulls on either side, but widening to at least double its previous width and three times the height. The tunnel came to another dead end, but it wasn't a wall that blocked their path this time.

"A door," Nadia stated, but even her voice was awe-hushed. Together, they made their way towards it, King's light stick illuminating their surroundings. Sid and Nadia's torches picked out more intricate details.

The 'door frame' stood three metres tall by four wide and looked like it was constructed from a single stone protruding out from the mountain's bedrock.

King's mind flashed back to the time he had spent with his father in the ruins of Tiahuanaco on the shores of Lake Titicaca in Bolivia. As a young man, he had spent hours staring up at the enormous Gateway of the Sun, a giant doorway constructed from a single piece of andesite. The image of the Staff Deity, a composite male/female entity portrayed holding a staff in either hand, had transfixed his father's attention for a time. He had sought links between Viracocha, the supreme, bearded god of the Andes, and the forebearers of his own African tribe, the Bouda.

This structure was identical in form to both the Gateway of the Sun and the Labyrinth entrance itself. But while their Bolivian counterpart was decorated with the Staff Deity and indecipherable patterns, the Labyrinth entrance and this doorway had both been stripped bare. Crude chisel marks offered the only suggestion that something more significant had once existed.

All that remained on the Labyrinth entrance was a single glyph, etched into the monolithic lintel after whatever had existed before had been erased: two feet encircled by a serpent.

However, the Andean civilisations possessed no form of written language, relying instead on the knotted cords of quipu to transmit information. As the tunnel construction suggested links to the Incans or their forbearers, most scholars considered the Labyrinth image to be just that: a picture for decoration rather than information transmission.

A few, including King, disagreed, suggesting that the image was a hieroglyph, all that remained of a vast, now erased, body of text. The feet symbol was identical to several epi-Olmec representations translated to mean 'lord'. This suggested un-documented cultural cross-contamination between the ancient peoples of Mesoamerica, two-thousand miles to the north of Sarisariñama, and the people of the Andes, one-thousand miles to the west.

If the feet were an epi-Olmec symbol, the snake encircling it might represent the famous Feathered Serpent god of various Mesoamerican religions such as Quetzalcoatl or Kukulkan. The symbol's transliteration was something like 'snake lord'. The other possibility was that it represented a river or boundary, demarcating the geographic extent of the Lord's rule.

King, however, had another theory and, as he stared at the same image now, his argument manifested itself. Here, the glyph was not some tiny tag like on the Labyrinth's entrance. Instead, it was a sprawling design carved into the face of the enormous slab that sealed the doorway. Its surface was also rough, covered with irregular grooves and notches from where some ancient vandal had destroyed what existed before.

"What did you reckon that symbol meant again?" Sid asked, already knowing the answer.

King's translation moved beyond the traditional forms of epigraphic decipherment. He and his father had spent decades travelling the world, analysing the abstract symbols and imagery found in rock art, cave paintings, folklore, oral traditions and other patterns. The academic world stated they held no narrative significance or information transmission:

it was art for art's sake.

But the Kings had identified a universality underlying such imagery, a shared, common interpretation held by humans, both ancient and modern. They argued that the 'Universal Motif Language,' or UML, was a 'symbolic language'. It was a unified method for the human mind to understand the world around them, irrespective of personal or cultural experience - something wired into the deepest, most primal parts of the brain and often accessed through shamanic trances and other Altered States of Consciousness.

Context was the key, the father and son team had argued, and the context of the hieroglyph he now studied left no doubt that it was a warning.

"Something happened here," he said. "Something so terrible that someone tried to erase all knowledge of this place from history." Within such a context, the serpent did not represent a river or a feathered god. It linked back to humankind's most instinctive, most primal interpretation of a snake: danger . . . death. Conjoined with the translation of feet as 'lord', its meaning was unmistakable.

"It means 'Lord of Death'," he whispered, sending a chill down his spine. "Read in context with the erased history, I think the overall message is something along the lines of 'Welcome to the House of the Lord of Death.'" He looked at his two companions. Even Nadia, who braved the chill of the tunnels with only a hi-vis vest over her form-hugging black t-shirt, folded her arms around herself, rubbing their goose-bumps.

"In other words," Sid added. "Keep out or else."

A high-pitched shriek echoed from above, and they all screamed, spinning around in a panic. Their lights shot up into an expanse above their heads, vanishing into the darkness. Long tendrils of roots, some as thick as a man's arm, hung out of the chasm, glistening with moisture and, as the trio peered up into the void, a single drip fell and splashed over Nadia's pale face.

She twitched, wiping it away with her arm, smearing bright red across her features.

King saw the look of horror on Sid's face as she recognised the substance. But saying the word out loud made his stomach clench with dread.

"Blood?"

3:

CARIMARA, BOLIVAR VENEZUELA

NATHAN Raine screamed as darkness consumed him.

It undulated around him like a physical entity, battering the windshield of his Huey as the helicopter hung above the jewel of Sarisariñama.

The view of the table mountain from above was usually spectacular. It was a two hundred square mile emerald island rising almost two and a half thousand metres above the rainforest. A halo of white cloud encircled it, its lush, forested summit basking in golden sunlight. Sheer cliffs guarded it on three sides while its north face slipped down a sharp incline, navigable by only the hardiest wildlife. Such isolation had permitted life on the mountain's summit to develop along its own evolutionary course. At the same time, the creatures inhabiting the jungle floor of its four gaping sinkholes were distinct even from each other and the life above.

The darkness spewed from the largest of the sinkholes, Sima Humboldt, a three hundred and fifty-metre-wide maw cutting through the jungle. It whipped out, filling the chasm before swallowing the expedition base camp. It moved like a swarm, a collective of individual back dots swirling around the tents, ripping through state-of-the-art equipment with electrical bursts and blossoming fireballs, possessed of one mind, one goal.

It dropped across the cloud forest like a tidal wave, washing through the trees. It extinguished all life in its path, pouring over the cliffs in a display more spectacular than any gushing waterfall. The deluge continued, roiling across the landscape as far as the eye could see. But Raine's immediate concern was the miasmic tendril that had whipped out from the mass, swatting at his helicopter like a fly.

The windscreen shattered, and the darkness engulfed him. The Huey swung out of control, spinning towards the ground, even as he wrestled to pull his limbs free of the tar-like substance. The darkness bit him, chewing his flesh like a ravenous beast, freezing and boiling him all at once.

His senses were overloaded.

The flash of a naked woman wrapping herself around him assaulted his mind. The touch of rock as she guided his hand, tracing his finger along a painting etched into a cave wall, grazing the skin from its tip. The frigid splash of water as he stumbled into a sapphire pool. An agonising explosion behind his eyes as the Huey struck the ground.

"Fuck me!" Raine cursed, shooting upright in his bed, squeezing his skull between his palms as though the pressure could relieve the agony of his burning brain. Bile raced up his throat, and he leapt out of bed, hurtling into the bathroom in time to throw up into the toilet basin.

Exhausted, he sagged against the bowl for several long minutes, calming himself. The vile-smelling contents of the toilet threatened another bout of vomiting, so he reached up and pulled the chain before staggering over to the sink. He ran the cold water tap, but it was still warm and held a yellow tint after sixty seconds. Deciding that was the best he would get, he splashed the liquid over his face and glanced in the mirror.

While his mop of black hair was admittedly

unkept on purpose, it stuck out in every direction this morning. His dishevelled reflection was in-keeping with the décor of the equally-dishevelled motel room. His normally sun-kissed skin was pale and drawn. The five o-clock shadow draped across his lower face held more silver than he liked. The bags under his startling blue eyes were bulbous and purple.

A moan came from the bedroom, and, looking down, his nakedness reminded him that he had company. However, his eyes settled on his muddy feet, making him frown. His hands were equally dirty, the tip of his index finger grazed and sore.

He staggered into the bedroom. It was a rundown mess like the rest of the motel and, indeed, the entire town. The bed was lumpy and smelt damp. Hideous lime-green wallpaper peeled off in long strips and shotgun pellets peppered the door like some monstrosity of the modern-art era. One window was boarded up with empty cereal packets.

The room's redeeming feature was the lithe shape that uncurled itself on the bed, stretching out her sinuous limbs. All she wore was a collar of bright beads, her golden-brown skin glistening with a sheen of perspiration. The overhead fan did nothing to cool her, merely stirring her black-as-night hair. Her eyelids, painted pastel blue, flickered open, obsidian orbs glancing at Raine, a smile splitting her face.

Raine didn't hide his arousal. He rubbed his temples, squinting in the pale light filtering through the grime-smeared window.

"What the hell did you say was in that moonshine?" he grumbled.

Maria's smile widened. She stretched back, exposing her nakedness. "It's my grandmother's secret recipe," she joked.

Raine plodded to the foot of the bed and crashed onto it. "I've got the hangover to end all hangovers," he grumbled, burying his face in his stale pillow.

Maria rolled onto her side, running a finger down his spine. She traced the pattern of tattoos that looped and swirled across his torso and arms, his only concession to his mother's Hawaiian heritage.

Despite feeling as though his head would explode, the contact sent pulses of electricity shooting through his limbs. He rolled to face her; she straddled a leg over his thigh, hooking a foot behind his knee, yanking the middle of his torso towards her.

"What happened last night?" he asked.

She raised an eyebrow. "If you don't remember, then one of us was doing something very wrong."

Raine grinned, flashes of their nocturnal activity invading his thoughts, blending with memories of his previous encounters with Maria.

He had encountered Maria over six months ago at the grungy dive calling itself Carimara's only bar. He had travelled from Caracas to Carimara for an overnight refuelling stopover every fortnight since. The following morning, he would continue to the UNESCO Expedition camp on Sarisariñama to deliver supplies before reversing the route two days later.

Carimara might as well have been the cesspit of the earth, nothing but a long road bordered on either side by dilapidated buildings. Less than a thousand downtrodden people populated it, a mixture of Spanish descendants, Mestizos and a handful of Ye'kuana. The latter had chosen to relocate from their traditional villages in search of western civilisation. Apart from fishing in the Carimara river, the town's lifeblood was Willy's Airstrip. This dusty, potholed track allowed oil prospectors, goldmine surveyors and more adventurous tourists access to the heart of Venezuela's southern rainforests.

Maria was the first Ye'kuana to have attended university in Caracas. But lack of funding and racial prejudice prevented her from securing a job in the city, forcing her to return to her homeland. There, she'd turned her anthropology degree to the study of her people, hoping to use it to represent the indigenous population in their dealings with the wider world.

It hadn't taken the bored pair long to discover a mutual interest in the only activity available in the town, returning to Raine's motel room on every stopover.

"Of course I remember that," he said, raising his hands to show her the dirt and minor injury. "But what about this?"

Maria glanced at his finger, pulling a concerned face. "Does it hurt?" She spoke as if to an infant, kissing the wound before taking his digit into her mouth, nibbling it. Then she thrust it deeper, sucking it while sliding so close to him that their bodies pressed against one another.

"Seriously," Raine said, extracting his finger. Maria smiled playfully.

"I took you on a Soul Flight, remember?"

Raine squinted, trying to recall the memory.

He remembered drinking several beers and cheap tequila in the bar, watching the sunset over the river, before Maria suggested doing something 'crazy'. Raine rarely objected to such an offer. He'd followed her out of town and down a well-worn track into the surrounding jungle.

"The elder women in my family have been *a'churi edamo* for generations," Maria had explained, leading him off the track and into the thick foliage. "A

". . . a shaman, or medicine woman, I guess you would say. But when I was eight, a storm triggered a mudslide, wiping out most of my village. Only my grandmother and I survived from my family. So, fearing the tribe would lose our ancestors' power after she passed away, she passed her knowledge on to me. As the youngest 'elder' in the history of the Ye'kuana, many of the tribe feared my so-called powers; I was an outcast."

"I'm sorry," Raine had replied. They had approached a cave, its entrance hidden behind a curtain of greenery and protected by a pool of water so clear that the silver orb of the full moon reflected from its mirror-like surface.

Maria had set about lighting a fire and, once roaring, poured a mixture of milky liquid from a flask into a pan. "One I prepared earlier," she had joked.

"When the government had a push to increase educational access to tribal societies," Maria continued, "the Central University of Venezuela offered a scholarship placement to the Ye'kuana. A council of elders decided that I'd benefit from the experience. In reality, it was a way of getting rid of me."

She brought the brew to a boil, and it gave off a sickly aroma that made Raine's head swim.

"One of the 'powers' my grandmother gave

me," Maria had continued, disdain in her tone, "was the ability to guide others on a Soul Flight . . . a vision quest. It is a way to explore one's inner soul, commune with the spirit world, and even look into one's future."

Raine had scrunched up his face, backing away. "I've always preferred the future to be unknown," he'd replied. "Makes life more exciting."

Maria had smiled. "Relax," she'd giggled. "You and I know that's a load of superstitious mumbo-jumbo." She shrugged. "One of the pitfalls of sending a shaman to uni, I guess: you educate them." She'd picked up the wooden spoon she'd been using to stir the mixture, allowing it to splash back into the container. "This is called *Yaddadi*. It's just a mixture of *ayahuasca* and a bunch of other psychedelic plants that stimulate parts of the brain to help you reach an ASC."

"A what?"

"An Altered State of Consciousness . . . a hallucination. That's all that happens when shamans use this stuff: they go on a massive 'trip', see some pretty crazy things, and then afterwards, they try to make sense of it all, claiming everything they saw had meaning. But it didn't," she had smiled, mischief twinkling in her eyes. "It's just one hell of a wild ride." Then she'd risen to her full height and pulled her vest-top over her head, undoing her belt to let her trousers glide down her slender legs.

"You have to be naked in this ritual?"

"No," Maria had replied, grinning. "But it's more fun. ASCs are renowned for their arousal responses," she'd teased. She scooped the *Yaddadi* into a plastic mug and held it to his lips with one hand while the other tugged at his belt. "And I don't know about you, but I'm already pretty damn aroused."

That was where Raine's recollection plummeted into a black hole. He remembered flashes of light, patterns and shapes swirling around him, the sense of falling, then of flying. He saw faces of people he knew and faces of strangers; he felt both bliss and terror as he travelled along a tunnel, emerging into blinding light.

Vague recollections of frolicking in the lagoon came back to him. He remembered making love to Maria within the embrace of the water, the kiss of silver moonlight travelling down the arc of her back as they writhed and groaned in pleasure. Then they splashed through the water into the cave, scrambling over rock, slipping and falling occasionally. They had found crude paintings on the walls, tracing them with their fingers.

"These are sacred to my people," she had whispered. "They tell of the *Ye'kuana Promise*; a time when the Evil Spirit is unleashed, and darkness smothers the land."

"Well, that explains the nightmare," Raine said now, lying against Maria on the bed.

"You remember?" Maria asked.

"Bits," he replied. "You?"

She smiled, her face full of warmth. "Bits," she admitted, then planted a kiss against his lips, grasping his buttocks to force him closer to her . . . into her. "The best bits."

The shrill cacophony of Raine's cell phone cut through their intimacy. Raine frowned but pulled away.

"Don't answer it," Maria said, thrusting her waist after him.

"I've got to," he said, rolling over to retrieve the offending device from his trouser pocket and looking at the number on the touchscreen. He stabbed at the answer button. "Hey Willy, this isn't a good time."

"Yeah, yeah, no doubt you're making love to a beautiful woman," the Icelander barked down the phone at him. "But, meanwhile, I've got another flight landing in fifteen minutes, and your pile of junk is still sat on my helipad."

"What are you talking about? I booked that pad until 1030," he scooped his discarded watch off the floor. "And it's now . . . 1012! Shit!" He threw his legs off the bed.

"Get that piece of crap off my runway in ten, or I'm charging you a whole extra day."

Raine glared at his phone screen as Willy cut the call. "Love you too, Willy," he grumbled, rubbing his eyes while fighting the urge to vomit again.

"You can't fly like this," Maria pointed out, frowning at him from her perch on the bed. "It's not safe."

"Yeah, well," Raine replied, searching for his discarded boxer shorts amidst the muddy clothes scattered around the room. "I don't exactly do 'safe'." He glanced under the bed, but there was still no sign of the elusive underwear. "How did we even get back here last night?" he asked. "And why do you look like the joys of spring while I feel like a grizzly's ass?"

Maria laughed in response, then scrambled across the bed to him, wrapping her arms around his chest from behind, nibbling his ear.

"You know, you could stay here and be 'unsafe' too," she suggested.

"You know I've got to go," he replied, struggling to rise. Maria clung to him, pulling him back down.

"No, you don't," she purred. "Stay here, with me, please."

"Oh crap," Raine sighed, pulling away and turning to look at her. "We agreed this was just a casual thing, remember? I'm not a commitment kinda guy."

Maria's face darkened. "I'm not asking you to marry me, Nate. I just don't want you to go to that mountain."

"Why?"

"It's dangerous."

Raine arched an eyebrow. "I think I can handle myself. I've been there enough times-"

"Please, Nate," Maria cut in. She bounded to her feet and stood before him, hands on his hips as though trying to guide his decision physically. "I'm not being needy or anything. I'm certainly not falling in love with you if that's what you're afraid of. If you stay here, we can do *casual* stuff all day and all night. But you mustn't go to that mountain."

Raine stared at the woman for a long moment, his icy eyes lost within her obsidian orbs, succumbing to temptation. Then he shook his head and resumed his search for underwear.

Maria sighed. "I'll find your clothes," she said, defeated. "And get you a cup of strong coffee. You jump in the shower."

Raine smiled at the woman as she shrugged on a white bathrobe. He took her in his arms and brushed a lock of hair from her face. "I'll be back in a couple of days," he reminded her, but she did not answer. He kissed her, then strode into the bathroom and scrambled into the shower cubicle. It was little more than a vertical coffin. His skin smeared against the glass panels even as the yellow-tinged, lukewarm water cascaded over his lean, muscular body. It did little to dismiss the jungle's oppressive heat, but the pounding of the water against his head eased the pain and made him feel more human.

He caught movement in the steamed reflection as Maria stepped into the bathroom doorway. For a moment, he thought that she would shrug off her robe and squeeze into the cubicle with him, and he decided that maybe Willy's extra day charge would be worth it. After all, he could just re-charge the fee to his employer, Sharpe Enterprises.

Then his eyes caught the glint of metal in Maria's hand.

Years of training slammed Raine's instincts into survival mode before his brain even registered what was happening.

A metal disk whistled from the Ye'kuana woman's fingers, smashing through the glass at neck height.

4:

THE LABYRINTH, SARISARIÑAMA TEPUI, VENEZUELA

SID gaped at Nadia.

"Blood?" she stammered, turning her attention back up the shaft. The dangling roots took on a new persona; the gutted innards of a dead creature, severed muscle and tissue oozing and bleeding. Beyond them, something moved, a shadow flitting in the glare of their combined artificial lights.

An instant later, dozens of bats exploded out of the dark hole, their frenzied divebombing shaking more blood from the gnarled roots. It rained down over the archaeologists, drenching them.

Sid huddled against the stone door as the winged denizens of Sarisariñama pummelled her, scratching and clawing, the pounding of their wings drowning out their screams.

She felt one slam against her head, knocking her senseless for a moment until the pain of claws scratching her scalp snapped her back to the moment. She reached around, trying to beat the creature free, but it was so tangled in her luscious black hair that it could not escape until King struck it with his light stick. The bat fell limp, allowing her to rip it free, along with a wad of hair, and she flung it away in disgust. It hit the floor, rolled, and then retook flight, joining the rest of its colony.

The swarm's collective momentum kept them hurtling out of the vertical chasm. They swung around the thrashing human invaders before vanishing around the bend in the corridor and out of sight.

Seconds after the furry deluge had begun, it was over.

Sid hunched alongside King and Nadia, trembling in a pool of blood as silence settled over them. The Russian broke it, her voice as calm as always.

"Not blood," she corrected Sid, as though nothing had transpired since her observation. She sniffed the red liquid that now covered them all.

"Water," she explained, "but with a heavy iron content creating a reddish hue."

Sid glared at her friend, rapid puffs of air haloing her as she tried to calm her breathing. Then she shifted her gaze to her boyfriend. "Hidden passageways that appear to bleed," she said, "lined with skulls, protected by killer bats and leading to the Lord of Death's lair . . . this place is really starting to creep me out, Ben."

But rather than offering the loving reassurance she sought, King pulled himself to his feet, placing a hand against the door. Pushing past the hurt of his neglect, something she had become accustomed to of late, she watched as his hand smeared in the condensation. His eyes caught the glare of her torch, gleaming as he stared at the stone slab as though looking through it.

"There's something on the other side of this door," he said reverently.

Sid and Nadia exchanged a frown.

"That is the commonly accepted function of a door," the Russian highlighted. "And they were not 'killer bats'," she added for Sid's benefit, "merely spooked ones."

"I was being poetic," Sid replied.

"Nor is the inanimate corridor bleeding."

"Again with the poeticness."

"That is not a word."

Sid huffed but returned her attention to King. He remained statue-like, palm against the door as though in communion with the monolith.

"Ben?" she said. He ignored her, eyes distant. "Ben!" she snapped, grasping his arm and whipping him back to reality.

"What?"

His startled expression frightened Sid; it was as though he was seeing her for the first time, as though he had left his body for a second, been transported to another place.

This place is creeping me out more than I thought, she reprimanded herself.

"We need to go," she told him.

"Not yet."

"Sid is right," Nadia came to her aid, holding out her arm to show numerous scratches. Tiny lacerations also peppered Sid and King's flesh, though none of them had been bitten. "We need to get these cuts sterilised immediately."

King was about to object, but Sid cut him off. "Karen was working around this section of the tunnel before she fell ill," she reminded him. "If those bats carry anything nasty, then McKinney stealing the limelight will be the least of our worries."

King opened his mouth, but Sid turned and

headed back up the tunnel before he could speak. Nadia fell into step beside her. She heard her boyfriend sigh in defeat but, after lingering a moment longer, he followed.

Sid had just rounded the sharp bend and glimpsed the demolished partition wall in her torch beam when a loud crack assaulted her ears. It was accompanied by a rumble beneath her feet.

"What now?"

"Move!" Nadia shouted, tackling her around the waist and hurtling them up the corridor as the ground dropped from under them. They hit the stone floor and rolled, turning just in time to see King jumping through a plume of dust, the thunder of crashing rocks filling the confined space.

"Ben!" Sid shouted, twisting to reach towards him, arms outstretched. His fingers brushed hers, but all she could do was watch as terror spasmed across his face.

Benjamin King dropped away from her, plummeting into dark oblivion.

5:

CARIMARA, BOLIVAR VENEZUELA

RAINE dropped to the shower base.

The spinning razor exploded out the far side before a fine thread attached to it snapped it taut and whipped it back to Maria.

Glass peppered Raine's back, only to be washed away by the water jet, swirling the pink cocktail of diluted blood down the rusted plughole.

"What the hell?" Raine shouted at his bedfellow. But Maria's eyes flashed with anger, and she unleashed her deadly weapon again. Raine dived backwards, crashing through the remains of the glass cubicle and sprawling on his back as the disk whizzed inches from his chest, snapped back to its owner, then lashed out again.

He hurled himself to his feet, slipping on the wet tiles, and threw himself over the toilet bowl to take shelter on its far side. The disc struck his protective barrier, chunks of porcelain ricocheting through the air.

"If this is about that whole commitment thing," he called to his attacker, "then I can change!"

The disc struck to bowl again, the impact shattering the far side so that toilet water gushed over the tiles.

"If you took your head out of your ass for one second," Maria shouted back, "then you'd realise the whole world doesn't revolve around you. Did you learn nothing last night?"

"Last night? I don't even remember most of last night!"

The disc screamed at him again, and Raine knew his cover wouldn't protect him. He darted out from hiding just as the metal blasted the rest of the porcelain apart. Then he skidded across the tiles to cower behind the far end of the long cupboard unit under the sink. Instead of shattering like the glass and porcelain, he hoped that the wood would grip the spinning razor of death, preventing Maria from snapping it back to her.

Maria came to the same conclusion and ceased fire. However, Raine could see her reflection in the mirror, wearing only a white robe. She poised like a viper, ready to strike the moment he stuck his head out of hiding.

"While I hate using clichés," Raine said, "can't we talk about this?"

"The time for talking is over," Maria replied. "I gave you a chance. I begged you not to go to Sarisariñama, but you would not listen. The alternative to this would have been much more pleasant for both of us."

"What's the big deal with me going there? There are almost a hundred other people there, and I don't see you trying to kill them."

"Darkness is stirring on the mountain; the Evil Spirit is awakening. I can feel it . . . I have seen it. It is my responsibility to stop it."

"By killing the guy you're sleeping with? How's that work? Besides, I thought you said all that prophecy stuff was a load of mumbo-jumbo?"

"I am an *a'churi edamo* of the Ye'kuana," she intoned. "Do you think I would forsake the sacred knowledge of my ancestors just because Western education has taught me the science behind the magic? I walk the line between this world and the next; I guided you on a Soul Flight, to show you that which I have seen, to show you the darkness in the hope that you would do the right thing."

Raine's mind flashed back to the terrifying vista he had witnessed in his nightmare: the darkness spewing forth from Sarisariñama and flooding the land. He felt a swell of anger towards his lover-come-wannabe-murderer.

"More like you drugged me. You planted the image in my head and manipulated me like some cheap cult leader softening his herd before a pill-popping grand finale."

"You saw the paintings in the cave, left by my ancestors," Maria said. "They tell of the Ye'kuana Promise, of how, many moons ago, when *nono*, the earth, was young, a balance existed between the natural and the supernatural."

Raine's mind shifted through the blurred images, recalling Maria gently tracing his index finger along the paintings on the wall, telling him the story.

"Then the Sun Father let three magical eggs fall," Maria continued now. "The first two eggs split open, and, from them, *Wanadi* and his brother were born. But the third egg did not break open but was smashed and deformed. Wanadi threw it into the forest where the Rain King found it. Taking pity upon the deformed egg, he cracked it open. *Cajushawa* spewed out upon the earth, bringing evil and death, misery and damnation. *Cajushawa* manifested himself in the form of a fanged face. With his army of *odosha*, his demons, he devoured the earth.

"But all was not lost," she concluded. "*Wanadi* left us, the Ye'kuana, to fight the demons. My ancestors locked them, and their lord, upon the mountain. There, the Face of *Cajushawa* remains to this day, making the sound *sari* . . . *sari* as he feasts upon the flesh of any who venture there."

"Yeah, I know the ghost story about how the mountain got its name," Raine shot back. "It's got some of the folks up there pretty spooked. But, moving on," he said calmly, then exploded in anger: "why the hell are you trying to kill me?"

"Because the Ye'kuana Promise tells of a day when the Rain King shall decide the fate of all humankind once more," Maria screamed back at him.

The Rain King, Raine remembered. His minds-eye traced the symbol: a pair of feet surrounded by a serpent. The serpent, he recalled Maria's words, brought death to many, but was also seen as a protector by the Ye'kuana.

"The Rain King is both the Lord of Death and the Lord of Life," Maria continued. "He is good and evil, right and wrong, black and white, light and darkness."

"Okaaay," Raine nodded. "But I return the conversation to my original question: why the *fuck* are you trying to kill me?"

"Because the darkness is stirring," Maria said, and Raine heard the unwavering conviction in her tone. "The fate of the world will soon rest in the hands of the Rain King; he will decide whether to flood the earth in light or drown it in darkness. But, if I can stop one half of the Rain King from going to the mountain, maybe I can change the fate of the world."

"You think I'm one half of the Rain King?" Raine laughed. "Just because of my name?" He stared at Maria's reflection, noting the determination on her face, knowing there was no reasoning with her. "Then where the hell is the other half?"

6:

THE LABYRINTH, SARISARIÑAMA TEPUI, VENEZUELA

KING smacked down onto the surface of the icy water, back first, blocks of the tunnel's floor splashing down alongside him. A cascade of dust and debris obscured his vision, followed by the panicked bubbles of his escaping breath.

He sank into the depths, thrashing his limbs as pressure assaulted his ears. But, just as he felt his natural buoyancy return him to the surface, one of the falling blocks slammed into his stomach. The impact doubled him over, the added weight shooting him like a torpedo towards whatever lay below. He gasped, sucking cold water into his lungs and inciting terror in his brain. He lost control of his instincts, unable to resist the urge to breathe.

Another block streamed down to strike his forehead with such force that it knocked the panic out of him. Blood blossomed as the masonry ripped a flap of scalp from his head; a kaleidoscope of shapes and colours whirled behind his eyes, growing narrower as he sank into the gloom.

He hit the bottom of the pool, the block on his stomach pinning him in place, the base crunching beneath him. The light stick he had been carrying hit the ground several metres away. Its diffused red glow mixed with the tint of the water's rich iron content, giving the impression of lying within a pool of blood. High above the surface, distorted by the ripples of the final pieces of falling debris, he saw the vague silhouette of the hole in the tunnel's floor, illuminated by the women's torches.

"Ben."

He heard a voice over the throbbing of his pulse in his ear, but it was neither of his companions. It was deep and soothing, calming him and allowing a surreal sense of relaxation to wash over him, even as water flowed down his throat and filled his lungs.

His father's voice always had that effect on him. It had from his earliest memories of lying in his arms, the big man chasing away the terror of a nightmare they both shared, until the last time King saw him alive.

It had been the two of them against the world for as long as King could remember; more than father and son, they were academic partners and best friends.

"What do you say, buddy?" Reginald King's face flashed before King's eyes now. It was a memory so vivid that it was as though he stood in Heathrow Airport again, saying goodbye to him one last time. *"Come with me. We'll find it this time. I'm certain. I can feel it in these old bones,"* he'd laughed.

Despite the situation, King could not stop himself from laughing also. He wanted nothing more than to take his father's proffered hand, follow him onto the plane and fly off with him on his latest adventure.

"Not this time, Dad," he had replied, the glassy look in his father's eyes more agonising than any dagger through the heart. *"I've spent my whole life looking, and where's it gotten me? I'm broke, discredited, and Sid . . ."* he had shaken his head. *"With the Sarisariñama Expedition, I've got a chance to put the UML to practical use, to decipher any images they find in those tunnels. If I can demonstrate its relevance on such a high-profile dig, maybe I can drum up support for our Progenitor Theory. And Sid, well, I've got to make another go with her, Dad. I love her, and she's*

sacrificed so much for my career, it's my turn to support her . . . Sarisariñama is her dream job."

Reginald had smiled then. It was a sad smile, knowing he had lost his partner in crime, but also a proud smile. *"I know, kid,"* he'd replied, voice raw. *"I know better than anyone that, once you find that special person, you have to sacrifice anything,* anything *for her."* His eyes had grown distant, full of self-recrimination, but he had pushed through it and dragged his son into a bearhug.

"Besides, what is it you always say?" King had added, unwilling to release his father.

"If you stop looking, you may find it," they intoned together, laughing.

"I love you, buddy."

"I love you too, Dad."

"See you in a few months."

With those words, they had parted ways. Three weeks later, Reginald's last communication had been a series of panicked text messages he'd sent as he'd tried to escape an attack on his expedition's basecamp. Four weeks after that, a Congolese guerrilla group had claimed responsibility for executing all members of the British-led archaeological team that had wandered into their territory.

"Ben," his father's voice pulled him back to reality, his guide even after death.

King twisted, dislodging the block from his stomach and floating free. He noted three dark voids cutting into the base of the walls and, to his left, a series of submerged steps rising to just below the surface. Pushing through his disorientation, he scrambled towards them, rolling onto his belly.

A skull glared up at him, mere inches below his face. But, as he stared back at it in horror, he watched as muscle, sinew, and skin regrew. It fleshed out the ghastly contours into a face he knew all too well, a face that haunted him every night.

General Abago Abuku sneered at King, placing the barrel of his gun against the centre of his forehead. Seconds ago, the same weapon had blasted his older sister's skull into a mush of exploding brain matter. Her body had crumpled onto the blood-soaked carpet alongside King's mother, their clothing torn and soiled, their bodies mutilated.

King stared up at the monster through the eyes of his three-year-old self. He screamed as the hot metal ring seared his flesh, branding him like an animal. His beaten, bloodied father sobbed as he lay tied up on the floor.

"No . . . please," he begged, snot, saliva, tears and blood pooling beneath his face.

This isn't real!

King slammed through the mental barrier and

pushed away from the skull, gliding backwards into more bones, crushing them beneath his weight. Unlike the tunnel above, these weren't just skulls but entire bodies, some mere shards, others fully formed. They carpeted the pool's base, sometimes several deep, tangled together in contorted poses of anguish, illuminated by the hellish glimmer of the blood-like water.

King forced his last reserve of self-calm to the surface and used it to swing his feet under him, boots crushing the skeletal remains, so he pushed off, kicking hard for the world above.

He burst out of the water and retched, emptying his lungs and gulping in the stale air. His heartbeat, amplified by water in his ears, echoed in his head while blood ran from his scalp, coating his face.

"Ben?!"

King glanced up, finding the hole in the ceiling where Sid and Nadia's worried faces peered through, gesticulating wildly. Their words seemed distant, incoherent as he tried to clear the water from his ears.

Treading water, he coughed again, waving at them to let them know he was okay. While it felt like he had been trapped underwater for a lifetime, he realised that only seconds had elapsed.

"I'm okay," he called up to them, but their concern didn't seem to lessen. Instead, it grew worse, sending a chill down King's spine. He wiggled his jaw again and felt an agonising pop in both ears, replaced by a sudden noise as though someone had just hit the unmute button.

"Get out of the water!" Sid and Nadia screamed at him. "Crocodiles!"

King gaped, his eyes making out three streamlined shapes below him, silhouetted by his submerged light stick.

"Shit!" he cursed, hurling himself forward and thrashing towards the steps he had seen earlier, hoping the reptiles didn't notice his movements. Once there, he scrambled to his feet in the waist-deep water and staggered to the nearest wall, pinning himself against it, hoping to diminish his profile. He kept his eyes on the deeper pool, watching the shapes beneath it.

One moved towards the submerged steps and appeared to grow as it ascended. King's body trembled so hard that he thought he would throw up. His head pounded, and he had to keep wiping blood out of his eyes. While the skull-lined tunnel was cold, the chamber he now occupied, the size of a football pitch, felt almost freezing. Soaked to the bone, he knew hypothermia was a danger.

One life-threatening menace at a time, Ben, he told himself, teeth clattering.

Without a sound, the crocodile broke the

surface, red water running over the rigid spines of its back and the contours of its head and snout. A single flick of its enormous tail propelled it towards the raised plinth at the top of the steps.

"Ben, do not move," a Russian accent warned from above.

In truth, however, he really didn't have a choice. Fear had frozen Benjamin King to the spot and all he could do was watch as the deadly predator shot through the water towards him.

7:

THE LABYRINTH, SARISARIÑAMA TEPUI, VENEZUELA

"**WE'VE** got to get him out of there," Sid gasped, staring through the hole in the tunnel's floor. She started forward as though she could do something, but Nadia grasped her wrist, halting her movements.

"Orinoco crocodiles are one of the less aggressive crocodilian species," the Russian genius told her, never taking her eyes off the reptile below. Illuminated from underneath, the creature's immense size became clear: it was over five metres long and weighed seven hundred kilograms at least.

"If Ben remains motionless, it may not see him in the dark. Even if it does, it may not be interested in him. It is cold down there, the water colder still; that a cold-blooded animal like a crocodile is down there at all is astonishing. The low temperature has hopefully made it lethargic."

Sid's dark eyes glanced across the hole at her friend, terror for her boyfriend etched upon her face. "And if it hasn't?"

Nadia raised an eyebrow and showed Sid her other hand. She gripped her flare gun in it, part of the expedition's standard-issue survival gear.

But Sid knew that however fast Nadia's reflexes were, the crocodile was faster. If it attacked, there was nothing anyone could do about it.

KING held his breath and watched the giant reptile glide through its domain into the shallow section of water in which he cowered. He pressed his back against the jig-saw patterned wall, flattening himself as much as possible.

A yellow eye caught the muted, rippling light, eliciting a wave of fear. A breath of air escaped King's lungs, cold vapour pluming around his head. The crocodile's eye flicked in his direction, and King fought to halt the quaking in his limbs.

The reptile's course shifted towards him, its motion slow, lazy almost, as though it was playing with him, taunting him, savouring the taste of the human's fear. But, with another flick of its tail, the creature's smiling snout whipped away, back on its original course, its giant body sailing past King.

King kept hold of his breath for a moment longer, until his scaled companion was several metres away, then let it go. He wrapped his arms around himself, rubbing warmth into his core, stealing a glance away from the crocodile to look at his surroundings.

Rippling red light illuminated the vast chamber, highlighting its architectural similarity to the Labyrinth.

Some of the blocks used in the Cellular Polygonal Masonry were much larger here than in the tunnels. Dark voids, mirror images of those he had seen underwater, sat at the top of the walls below the ceiling, with trickles of water running from them. Slithers of slime suggested they sometimes spewed more significant quantities of water into the chamber. King thought again about his suggestion of the Labyrinth being little more than a water management system.

Perhaps this chamber is some giant well, he considered.

A horizontal layer of dried slime, running around the room's circumference one metre above his head, gave credence to that theory. It suggested the water level was inconsistent, rising and falling perhaps in line with the rainfall on the mountain's summit.

"Ben? Are you alright?" Sid called to him.

King glanced up, nodding, his mouth dry. He wiped more blood from his eyes. "I'm fine," he lied, steadying his voice and retrieving a torch from one of his waistcoat pockets. "I'm . . . I'm in a chamber of some sort," he reported, thumbing it on. The beam cut through the gloom, hitting the far wall as he tried to orient himself, picturing his position within the tunnel system while keeping a wary eye on the lurking crocodile.

The incline of the skull-lined corridor was sharp. It doubled back on itself to the monolithic door they had discovered, which, King guessed, lay submerged under the pool's deep end.

Panning the torch beam up and across the ceiling, he noted the vaulted roof, two ribs containing the collapsed tunnel floor. He continued the torch's sweep, turning back to track the investigative crocodile as it glided around the opposite end of the chamber.

"Shit!" he yelped, jumping in terror.

"Ben? What's happening?" Sid demanded.

"I have a rope," Nadia added, though King could no longer see her face above. "We'll get you out of there."

"I'm okay," King replied, settling himself. Another shudder passed through him as his torch beam played across what had caused his fright: more skeletons. This time, they were not just mortared into place on the walls but were positioned with meticulous precision. Some were polished into points, others smoothed. Yet more were carved with intricate detail, so they created a single piece of art: the mosaic of a giant face covering the enormous wall opposite the monolithic doorway.

The face was hideous, an inhuman monster snarling, eyes reflecting cold malevolence within the beam of his torch, mouth agape, jagged teeth bared. Within the gaping maw lay a single skeleton, and, focussing his torch upon it, the sparkle of metal beckoned.

Something splashed in the water behind him, and King spun, torch held aloft like a weapon, ready for the fight of his life.

"Ben, grab on," Sid called as King's eyes focussed on the source of the splash: a rope tossed from above. It hung just a metre beyond where the plinth he stood on shelved off, meaning he would have to jump onto it to prevent another swim in the deeper pool with the crocodiles.

"Hurry, Ben," Nadia urged.

King watched the more adventurous croc complete its circle of the plinth and descend back into the pool's deep end. Then he started towards the edge of the submerged platform.

"If you stop looking, you may find it."

His father's words rang through his skull, as clear as the day he had spoken them. But the memory was far more vivid this time. For a fleeting second, King could picture the moment in exact detail: the untidy living room, his toys strewn amongst piles of his father's books, rays of sunlight beaming through the grimy windows, Reginald King lounging back in his worn armchair, covered by a brightly coloured throw, buried inside some archaeological textbook.

"But Dad," Benny had whined, having lost his favourite toy: a superhero mask. *"I want to be a superhero. I want to save the world."*

Instead of scolding him, his father had laid down the thick tome he had been reading. He'd looked at him, eyes teary with the misplaced pride of a father for the actions of a son yet to be committed. Hope for the young boy to become a greater man than he.

His father dropped onto his knees in front of him and grasped his shoulders. *"You will be, Benny,"* he had said with conviction, his voice serious. *"One day, I do not doubt that you will. But,"* he added, a mischievous smile spreading across his lips. *"You don't need a mask to be a hero."* His father's smile had always been infectious, lighting up his entire face. Despite little Benny's attempts to remain grumpy, his own face broke into a mirror image.

"Especially," his father pressed, eyes glinting, *"in the face of such a diabolical villain as . . ."* He had reached behind him, whipping the throw from his tatty armchair, swirling it about himself like a cape while unleashing a manic, supervillain laugh. *"Me!"* he finished, lunging at his son. Benny had fought against him, giggling as his father's fingers found his ribcage, digging in with a knee-crumbling tickle, their modest home filled with laughter.

"If you stop looking, you may find it."

King halted, rubbing his eyes to relieve the pain in his head and wiping more blood away. "Hang on a sec," he shouted up to Sid and Nadia before turning and wading through the water towards the monstrous face. He moved as silently as possible, wincing as each footfall crushed the bones beneath him.

"Ben, you need to get out of there!" Sid shouted.

"This might be your only opportunity," Nadia added.

But King ignored them, staring up at the giant art installation, created out of human bones, that towered above him. It glistened like some caged demon, basking in the hellish red light.

The same sense of awe that had overcome him when standing outside the monolithic doorway returned. Yet, it was more than just awe; it was as though he was being drawn, pulled towards it.

Ignoring his archaeological training, he used the joins between the bones as finger and toeholds. Then he hauled himself up to peer into the fanged mouth.

The skeleton he had seen from below lay slumped on its side, curled up in the foetal position as though the individual had died in terror or agony . . . or both. Its back was against the far wall of the tiny alcove, its knees bent, legs folded under it, face buried between skeletal fingers.

As he expected, much of the skeleton had decomposed. Still, it was far more intact than he would have thought possible for its likely age and, most surprising of all, fragments of clothing still clung to the yellowed bones. Scanning his torch over it, the most shocking thing was a triangular band of thin gold sitting around the skull, still attached to small chunks of felt-like material.

"Ben," Sid called again from above. "Hurry!"

"What have you found?" Nadia asked, more interested in his discovery than his welfare.

"A skeleton," he shouted back up.

"Wow," Sid mocked. "It's not like we haven't seen any of them embedded in the walls!"

"This one's different," King explained. "It's a complete skeleton. And, judging by its clothing, he wasn't from around here."

"Where do you think he came from?" Nadia asked, a hint of excitement breaking through her icy demeanour.

"Europe."

"Conquistador?" Sid asked. The Spanish Conquistadors had penetrated deep into the Amazon in their ruthless quest for gold.

"Not unless conquistadors wore tricorns," he replied.

"Tricorns?"

"There are fragments of clothing on it, including a piece of triangular gold gilding; I think it was the decoration on an expensive hat . . . a tricorn."

As further evidence that his unmoving companion was not local, he noted a sword lying next to it; dropped, he assumed, at the time of death. Yet, any self-respecting archaeologist knew the ancient people of the Americas did not develop metal weapons. Instead, they relied on stone, bone and wooden instruments to wage war.

However, a metal sword wouldn't have been out of place on the remains of a conquistador. The more 'advanced' steel weapons were one of the driving forces behind the successful conquest of the New World. Yet, this weapon wasn't some intricate rapier, the favoured weapon of the invading Spanish, but was a heftier, more brutal instrument.

Its handle was chunky, the hilt stocky, its long, straight blade tarnished.

King looked towards the figure's left hand. With mounting excitement, he noted a matching dagger still clasped between skeletal fingers.

His eyes narrowed at his unexpected discovery as an idea blossomed in his mind.

"If you stop looking, you may find it."

It was probably not what he was hoping for, he knew. Yet, he was confident that this was no conquistador. Everything else seemed to fit his developing theory, even if only circumstantially: the circa. 18th Century sea-faring attire, the matching sword and dagger...

But then, any 18th Century seafarer may have carried a matching set of weapons, he told himself, trying to keep a sense of realism.

He drew a cloth from a waistcoat pocket and, propping himself against the wall, rubbed at a small section of the sword. At first, the grime on the blade wouldn't shift, but eventually, the metal shone through, reflecting golden in his torch beam as he rubbed harder.

No, not gold.

"Brass," King gasped, letting go of his perch and splashing back into the pool.

"Ben!" Sid called. "What's going on? Are you okay?"

King grunted something affirmative at his girlfriend, never taking his eyes from the skeleton within the monster's mouth.

"Is it you?" he asked as if expecting the dead man to answer. Even as he felt certainty taking hold in the pit of his stomach, he fought to slow his breathing, to focus his mind.

It's impossible, he told himself. But then, shining his torch back at the human remains, something in its right hand caught the light, glinting as it was pressed against the unblinking skull.

He re-scaled the wall to peer through the jagged teeth of bone into the alcove once more. He reached towards the dead man's face, prising brittle fingers apart, his own brushing cold metal.

"The Moon Mask is real," his father told him as they sat together around a campfire, surrounded by the standing stones of Wassu.

"I don't know where it is!" his father screamed as General Abuku held a gun to his son's head.

"If you stop looking, you may find it."
"I love you, buddy."
"Ben!"

A wave of nausea slammed into King, and he almost fell off the wall again, taking hold of a giant tooth to steady himself. Coupled with the blood pouring from his head wound, the pounding behind his eyes and the disorientation, he knew his injury was more significant than he had admitted to Sid and Nadia. Yet, he could not move or call up to them. Instead, his eyes fixed on the circular slab of metal he took in his hand, a microcosm of the domineering façade on the wall.

"Ben!" the warning came again, but it was not in his head this time.

He glanced around just in time to see a torpedo shooting through the red-lit water towards him, bursting out of the depths, jaws wide.

8:

CARIMARA, BOLIVAR VENEZUELA

"THERE is a point where magic and science collide."

The words echoed through Maria's mind as she stood in the doorway to Nathan Raine's bathroom, the American sheltering at the end of the long wooden under-sink unit. Water gushed from the shower and the smashed toilet, pooling around Maria's bare feet, but she ignored it, standing firm.

I cannot allow the Rain King to escape, she vowed.

The only sign of any inner conflict was her white knuckles as she squeezed the leather sheath of her *okoiaki*, her crown. Such headdresses were reserved for high-status ritual use by men. But, after she had survived the mudslide that had wiped out her village and become the youngest *a'churi edamo*, they had granted her a special *okoiaki*. It was a metal disk, its perimeter sharpened to a razor's edge. A polished leather sheath, decorated with beads and feathers, protected her palm from being sliced open. It was attached to a fine cord of woven *oaxica* leaves, the elasticity of which snapped it back to the bracelet she wore over her hand and wrist.

She had honed her use of the chakram-like weapon while hunting and defending her people from attacks by neighbouring tribes. This was the first time she had used it in what many of her Western associates would consider outright murder.

No, that's not what this is, she told herself.

She had tried to make Raine understand. She had even shown him the sacred cave where her ancestors had left their warning, guiding him on a Soul Flight to show him the future that awaited should he return to the mountain. But his combination of ignorance and arrogance led her to such drastic measures.

She could see it in the reflection of his ice-blue eyes in the mirror now. A shift in the way he looked at her, transforming from respect for her academic background to humouring her primitive belief in magic. She had encountered the same look of something verging on pity many times at university. At the same time, contrarily, her tribe viewed her newfound scientific reasoning similarly. It was as though the Rain King's duality existed within her also, the same battle between right and wrong, light and dark, good and evil, magic and science.

Perhaps that's why it's my destiny to stop the Rain King from unleashing the Evil Spirit.

One person, however, had helped reconcile those two halves of herself. He'd showed her that she could retain her traditional beliefs and the power they enthused her with while understanding that power from a scientific perspective.

Doctor Henri Moreau, a visiting academic at the University of Venezuela in Caracas, was the world's foremost neuro-theologist. He'd spent years delving into the neurological basis for religious and spiritual experience. His words had spoken to her torn identity- a shaman and a scientist. Until his advice, Maria had convinced herself that one could not be both.

"This is not a mutually destructive process, as many would have you believe," she remembered him saying. He'd stood in front of an auditorium of archaeology, anthropology, theology and neurobiology students.

"In Western arrogance, we assume that the superiority of science destroys magic. While to many traditional cultures, science is but another form of magic, a way of understanding magic or, at worst, is little more than a false religion of sorts. But I believe this collision between science and magic is a beautiful thing rather than some apocalyptic showdown. And it happens right here," he had tapped his head, "in the human brain. I call it the neurotheological sweet spot.

"Science can explain how one achieves an Altered State of Consciousness through a chemical reaction in the brain, triggered by substance taking, starvation, pain, or sometimes the result of a head injury. We think of these episodes as hallucinations . . . and they can be good fun," he had grinned, earning a few chuckles from his audience.

"In controlled environments, of course," he added, his French accent rolling off his tongue. "Many young people experiment with magic mushrooms, for instance. Even that state you get to when you're completely pissed, and you only remember snippets of how you got home last night. Or who the naked person lying next to you is- and we've all been there." He had stared at the crowd, a charismatic grin on his face, earning more laughter. "That could be considered a minor 'Altered State of Consciousness'.

"Indeed, during many ASCs, the *nucleus accumbens*, part of the so-called 'pleasure centre' of the brain, is stimulated. This makes the experience a sensual one, and orgasm itself can trigger ASC as well as being a umm . . . shall we say 'final destination'?"

Moreau's good humour brought his audience's attention from mildly bored to thoroughly engaged. It didn't hurt that the rather dashing, dark-haired Frenchman talked about his people's most clichéd association.

"Of course, there are some dark sides to ASC, certainly in Western culture. Substance abuse is the most obvious. But the physical and psychological benefits are being explored with greater enthusiasm by the scientific community. Some even suggest that controlled ASC could be used to treat cancer.

"Different stimuli trigger different ASC experiences. Some can be ecstatic highs; others can be mental lows. Some can be vivid recollections, almost photographic in their accuracy. Others can be fantastic in their imagery of monsters, lovers, flying or sinking, for instance. Many studies are being conducted into the different chemical responses in the brain to 'map' ASC experiences. But, at the moment, I would say each experience is different for each individual, primarily based on that individual's cultural and environmental stimuli.

"And here we come to the crux of my statement, to that point where science collides with magic," Moreau had announced. "If one experiences an ASC due to an injury, we talk about near-death experiences, travelling through a tunnel towards the light, or of one's life flashing before one's eyes. These 'visions' are triggered by complex reactions going on up here," he tapped his head again. "But, is that light at the end of the tunnel nothing more than an ocular illusion? Or does it mean something? Did your whole life flash before your eyes, or was it merely a particularly poignant moment that replayed itself, and if so, why? Or, did what you saw blend reality with fantasy, like the result of watching a horror movie before bed and dreaming of yourself getting stabbed to death in the shower, accompanied by iconic music, of course? Or is it perhaps a message, a portent, a glimpse of the future?

"Science can't and, in my opinion, will never have a definitive answer to these questions.

"I don't believe in God," he had clarified, "but I do believe in the power of the human brain, in its untapped potential. Stemming largely from a personal experience, I started my career trying to disprove the notion of Extra Sensory Perception – things like retrocognition or precognition, telekinesis, remote viewing. These facets of ESP can arguably result from

Altered States of Consciousness, especially in traditional societies. I argued that even well-documented ESP cases are grounded in science. They are mere imaginative 'blips' of the psyche. But, like many of my peers, as I peeled back the layers of the brain's complexity, I have been unable to complete my task of disproving ESP. The brain's power, you see, goes beyond science and into magic.

"Shamanism," he had continued, bringing the subject into starling focus for Maria as she sat in the hall, "is tied to ASC and ESP. Specifically through claims of entering a trance and seeing the future, or of communing with spirits or ancestors. To you and me, it might sound preposterous. But is it?

"The physical and neurological process of a shaman's ASC is identical to any other. But shamans and traditional societies have learned to understand and interpret their 'visions', often in incredibly accurate ways."

Intense, dark eyes had peered into the throng of faces, and Maria remembered feeling as though they had singled her out.

"Will there be a drought?" he asked, then shrugged. "Could you or I answer that? Probably not.

"But I spent two years living with a community of San Bushmen in South Africa. I watched their shaman enter trances on fifteen separate occasions.

On fourteen of them, his predictions of the near future came to pass." Moreau held up a hand to halt an explosion of dubious responses from his audience.

"On the twelfth trance I witnessed him awaken from, he told his people to prepare for a drought." Moreau had paused, ever the showman, building suspense.

"It was fourteen months until the next drop of rain fell," he said, breaking the spell. "But his people took the shaman's advice and stockpiled their water supply, surviving the drought while their neighbours perished. Is that magic?"

Several heads had nodded, only to snap to attention at Moreau's next word.

"No," he said. "No, that wasn't magic - it was the neurotheological sweet-spot, the point where magic and science collide.

"You see," he had continued, "the shaman was an old man who had lived through an even more terrible drought in his youth. Before entering his trance, without knowing it, his environment had fed his brain snippets of information: a lack of grazing animals in the area, a sudden abundance of drought-tolerant flora, a quickened pace of fruit production on the trees, faster evaporation of morning dew. All of these are precursors to drought but were so mild at that point that no one could have consciously noticed them.

"The chemical reaction in the shaman's brain during his ASC, however, highlighted these environmental stimuli; that is the scientific process at work. The magical process is the spiritual journey he went on, guided, he told me, by an antelope spirit who was fleeing the coming disaster. Did the collision between science and magic take the form of the neurological response to a theological process? Or," he asked his audience, "was it a theological response to a neurological process?"

Moreau had shrugged then, the point made. "Science and magic," he had concluded, "can, and do, coexist."

Now, Maria took strength from those words. She, too, understood her neurological response to the legend of the Rain King and the resurrection of the Evil Spirit. She had been told the story from an early age; she had seen the paintings her ancestors had made. When she had met Nathan Raine and Benjamin King, one of the scientists he was ferrying to Sarisariñama six months ago, she understood the significance. Cajushawa's second coming was at hand.

Hoping to stop it peacefully, as was the way of her people, she had guided Raine on his Soul Flight, only to realise she was out of time. She understood the science of how her brain interpreted her cultural stimuli during their shared ASC, producing vivid visions of darkness encompassing the land. Raine had also seen this; she remembered him telling her. Yet he couldn't look beyond the science, couldn't see its collision with magic.

"Benny?" Raine gasped at Maria's revelation of the second half of the Rain King's identity. "You think Benny King is the other half of this mythical figure . . . and that he's the good half and I'm the bad?"

"It is said the Rain King will have a choice," Maria told her lover. "I have given you that choice, and you have chosen poorly."

Raine frowned. "Isn't that a quote from The Last Crusade?" he asked.

"Stay here with me," Maria said, imploring him to see reason. "Or go," she added. "Leave this place and never return. I don't want to hurt you, Nate."

"Then put down your death-frisbee, and we'll kiss and make up."

The American's arrogance steeled Maria's heart. She braced herself, stance shifting, struggling to get a better shot at Raine's position. He had nowhere to go, and they both knew it.

"I have a duty, a responsibility," she told him. "To my people and the world."

"This is crazy," Raine snapped. "You're basing cold-blooded murder on superstition and coincidence."

His words cut into her resolve. Part of her knew he was right, knew this was crazy, but she shook her head.

"I'm sorry, Nate, but I will not let you go to that mountain."

Raine's eyes locked onto hers through their reflection in the mirror, sadness sweeping through the blue orbs that she had lost herself inside of so many times. But, like a lake freezing over, an icy hardness descended on them.

"Then I'm sorry too, Xena," Raine said, leaping into action.

Moving far quicker than Maria expected, Raine sprang out of cover, hurling himself over the sink. She threw her *okoiaki,* but Raine dropped to his belly, sliding across the bathroom furniture. The spinning disk whirled above his body, even as he threw something into the air.

Maria's eyes snapped onto the object, taking a split second to recognise it as a deodorant aerosol with a flaming wick attached to it.

The can exploded at the top of its arc, the fireball carried aloft on a puff of sickly-smelling gas. It slammed into her and hurled her out through the doorway.

Before she could recover, Nathan Raine, the

man prophesied to destroy the world, made his move.

9:

THE LABYRINTH, SARISARIÑAMA TEPUI, VENEZUELA

"SHIT!"

Without thinking, King hauled himself up and squeezed between the razor-sharp teeth of the demonic face, snatching his feet inside the bony prison as the crocodile's jaws slammed shut behind him.

The crocodile rebounded off the bone-encrusted wall, taking chunks of the macabre decoration with it. It thrashed about in the water and launched at King again. Its powerful snout smashed the bone teeth, its own much deadlier ones gnashing at him. He curled in the alcove's corner, mimicking the skeleton's petrified foetal position.

Is this how you died? he wondered.

The crocodile's angle of attack was awkward, preventing it from fully opening its jaws or seeing what it was doing. But King knew one lucky munch was all it would take for it to be over.

Above the throbbing of his heartbeat in his head and his cries for help, he heard Sid and Nadia shouting to him, desperation in their tones, helplessness.

The crocodile's mass dragged it down the wall again, affording King a moment's breather. He glanced out at the chamber, noting the rope still dangling a third of a football pitch away. More black shapes darted through the water, erupting out of the submerged tunnels he had seen earlier, breaking the surface and thrashing about, their previous lethargy replaced by bloodlust.

So much for being a less aggressive species of crocodilian, King thought with bitterness, having overheard Nadia's earlier comment.

King's tormentor struck again, as if to prove the Russian wrong – something only a five-metre-long crocodile dared do. This time it propelled itself with such force that most of its head ended up inside the alcove, the base of its lower jaw resting on King's body. The tremendous power of its opening jaw threatened to crush the archaeologist. All King could do was land a handful of panicked punches to the side of its head.

It hurt his fist more than the living dinosaur.

To King's utter astonishment and horror, the leathery monster's eye fixed onto him, shining with intelligence as it changed tactics, twisting its head to snap at him sideways. The jaws closed, and King screamed as several teeth strafed his chest, ripping his shirt and flesh before punching a hole through the lapel of his waistcoat.

Scrambling in the darkness, King's hand wrapped around the hilt of the skeleton's discarded sword. Acting on instinct, he swung it at the side of the beast's head, splitting its armoured skin and hitting bone. Dark blood spurted over him as the crocodile threw itself back into the water just as an explosion of blinding light seared King's retinas.

"Ben! Quick!"

Blinking away the afterburn of Nadia's flare, King saw the Russian hanging upside down from the rope, gun still in hand. The firework-like explosion inside the gloom of the confined space stunned the chamber's snappy denizens, many of them thrashing about on the surface, blinded and in a panic.

King's limbs refused to move, to obey him. He curled up, trembling, his blood mixing with his reptilian attacker's.

"Now!" Nadia yelled, and King realised it was his only chance; the crocodiles' distraction would only last a moment.

Tucking the mask inside his waistcoat, taking an odd sense of comfort from its touch, he summoned the last of his energy reserves. He bolted out of the alcove, splashing into the blood-red pool. He didn't bother with stealth anymore but ran as fast as possible, sloshing through the water towards the rope.

"Ben!" Sid's scream echoed through the chamber, but King tried to ignore it, and the shape speeding towards him just below the surface.

Legs pumping, he hit the top step of the submerged stairway and flew towards the rope. Even as his hunter burst from the pool behind him, he realised his hands would fall just short of salvation. But Nadia reached out and grasped King's wrists with vice-like strength. Her exposed, solid core muscles tensed as she hung upside down, her legs wrapped around the rope like a gymnast, taking their combined weight. Momentum swung them over the pool to slam into the jigsaw-puzzle walls and rebound off them, back towards the crocodile as it splashed down.

"Grab the rope!" Nadia shouted, agony coursing across her upside-down face, her dark hair draping around King. He did as instructed and watched as the Russian flexed in the middle. She uprighted herself before scrambling up the rope, King right behind her.

Only a metre from safety, a commotion below caught his attention.

He glanced down to see the crocodiles dash under the water, no longer driven by bloodlust but by survival instincts. The object of their fear became clear. Something hurled one of their brethren out of the pool, snapping and thrashing, tail smacking the water in a frenzy. Thick, silky coils wrapped themselves around it.

The crocodile's left eye gazed up at King, revealing a horrific and bloody slash across the side of its head. It surrendered to its attacker and slid beneath the surface.

"Ben, come on."

King snapped his head around at the sound of his father's voice from above, but it was Sid who leaned over the hole, reaching a hand towards him.

Blinking thoughts of his father from his mind, King clambered the rest of the way to safety, taking his girlfriend's hand and rolling away from the jagged edge. Wiping blood from his eyes, he glanced down to note that the chamber was still once more: the crocodiles, and their tormentor, had vanished, leaving nothing but a suffused red glow rippling across the chamber.

Dazed, King fell back against the skull-lined tunnel wall, teeth chattering and limbs shaking. Sid and Nadia's movements seemed slow and surreal as they rushed around him, wrapping him in a foil blanket from their first-aid kit and mopping blood from his face. He saw their mouths open and close as they spoke to him, worried faces intruding into his field of view. But all he could hear was the beat of his racing heart as he retrieved his prize from within the folds of his torn leather waistcoat, smiling at the demonic face leering back at him as though it was a long-lost friend.

Three words formed on his lips, escaping as little more than a breath: "The Moon Mask."

10:

CARIMARA, BOLIVAR VENEZUELA

RAINE was ready for the detonation of his improvised grenade. He had hastily fashioned it from a can of deodorant with a broken-off piece of an incense stick, found in the far cupboard, along with a box of matches.

He rolled off the counter and splashed into the pool of water. The fireball singed his naked flesh, but he rolled over, cooling any burn instantly, before scrambling to his feet. He dashed out of the bathroom just as Maria rolled onto her side, the front of her bathrobe smouldering, her hair singed, and her face reddened. Her burn was superficial, but the real fire raged behind her eyes.

She dragged the extended cord of her weapon towards her as Raine lunged out of the bathroom and over the bed. He snapped up his bathrobe and swirled it around his shoulders while scrambling for his gun, holstered in his discarded trousers. But Maria recovered before he could reach them, her frisbee of death whistling towards him.

Raine fell back, his hand wrapping around his phone but nothing else of use. Maria's spinning blade shot towards him again, but he jumped over it, landing on the bed and using its spring to catapult him towards the window. The cereal boxes covering it crumpled under the impact, and Raine dropped, with a painful thump, two metres to the false roof of the motel's reception area below.

Stealing a glance up, he noticed Maria's lithe form appear in the window, obsidian eyes glaring at him. But, instead of unleashing her weapon as he expected, she let out a high-pitched whistle.

Movement on a rooftop across the dusty street caught Raine's attention. A figure appeared there, head wrapped in a halo of feathers, a large blowpipe pressed to his lips.

"Crap," Raine cursed as a dart, undoubtedly poisoned, shot towards him. He rolled down the ceiling and fell from it, landing on the canvas roof of an old pick-up truck. The motel owner, a skinny man in a yellow-stained once-white vest, ran out from his reception desk, yelling at him in Spanish.

Raine ignored him, jumped to the ground and swung open the 4x4's door. Another dart danced off the metal, followed close behind by an arrow from the opposite direction.

Raine hauled himself inside, even as the motel owner tried to drag him back out, receiving a headbutt as payment.

In such a small backwater, with a single road leading into it from the north, vehicular security was minimal. Raine flipped open the sun visor and caught the set of keys that spilt out, ramming them into the ignition. He slammed the 4x4 into gear and skidded out of the motel parking lot in a plume of dust.

He gained speed as he punched up through the gears, racing along the potholed road and scattering the town's few residents. He saw more Ye'kuana appear along the rooftops, their traditional attire at odds with the shantytown's décor. They moved with surprising agility, springing across chasms between buildings while hurtling a barrage of darts and arrows at the fleeing vehicle.

A flash of white caught Raine's attention, and he glanced up to see Maria there, racing along with her brethren, wearing nothing but the bathrobe.

His momentary lapse in concentration sent Raine hurtling through a tower of bird cages stacked along the side of the road. They flew up and over the bonnet, smashing to unleash the fluttering poultry within and obscuring his vision. He crashed into the wooden veranda of the town's bar.

Raine spun the wheel to the left, powering away from the impact even as the wooden structure crumpled down on top of him.

The end of the town came into view ahead, a mile of bumpy track leading to Willy's airfield. But, even slamming pedal to metal, with the speed of his pursuers and their agility in the jungle terrain, he knew they wouldn't be far behind.

He pulled his phone from his bathrobe's pocket, hitting redial and the hands-free button just as a figure came into view, blocking his path with an enormous bow. He unleashed an arrow, and Raine spun the wheel to the right as it smashed through the windscreen, the glass shattering over his exposed body. Before he could regain control, the Indian broke into a sprint, running towards the racing vehicle.

Raine tried to avoid impact, but his attacker leapt into the air, landing on the 4x4's bonnet to thrust a knife inside.

Snapping his head away, Raine veered the

pickup across the road to slam into the 'Welcome to Carimara' sign, the dilapidated board splintering on impact as he left the town.

"Raine?" Willy's voice barked through his phone. *"You've got three minutes!"*

"Willy!" Raine shouted back, whipping up an arm to deflect the Ye'kuana man's next attack. "Get my engines started!"

"What am I now? Your personal assistant?"

The Indian hauled himself deeper into the cab, getting a better angle of attack. He grasped the steering wheel, turning the jeep towards the jungle running along the side of the road. Raine fought back, straightening the vehicle before it slammed headfirst into the unforgiving trunks. He still lost his wing mirror in another shower of glass.

"Willy! I don't have time to argue. Just do it!"

The Icelander paused. *"What's going on?"*

Raine threw a punch at his attacker's face. "I'm being chased by a whole army of Indians with arrows and poisoned darts and need to get out of Dodge, pronto."

"What did you do this time?" Willy sighed.

"I slept with one of their Elders."

"Dude, that's gross." The forced Americanism was lost in the Icelandic twang.

"She was a young Elder," Raine corrected.

"Oh, you mean Maria," Willy laughed.

"Yeah," Raine groaned, lashing out at his attacker's face. "I knew there was something about her." The Indian slashed his knife at Raine's neck. "Hang on. You knew she was a shaman and didn't tell me?"

"She's not just a shaman, Nate. She's like the shaman, you know; the shaman to end all shamans, prophesied to avert the end of days or some shit."

"Yeah, I heard something about that."

"Besides, I didn't know you were going to sleep with her," Willy protested. *"Although, in hindsight, I should have seen it coming."*

Raine rolled his eyes and then let go of the steering wheel, grasping his attacker by both his ears and slamming their heads together. Blood gushed from the other man's nose as Raine chucked him back through the shattered windscreen. He rolled off the bonnet.

"Just do it, Willy!" he barked at his phone. Glancing in his rear-view mirror, he saw a small army of scantily clad but heavily armed men racing after him, led by Maria. "I'm coming in hot!"

The narrow avenue the road cut through the rainforest opened out just ahead, the airfield hugging the left-hand side. The propellers of his Huey slowly spun as the Icelander whisked through an emergency pre-flight sequence, warming the engines. It relieved Raine to see that Willy had been following instructions while exchanging banter.

Raine threw the pickup off the road, crashing through the airfield's gates and under the faded, flaking sign featuring a distasteful, artistic interpretation of the owner's name blended with a fixed-wing aircraft. He raced towards his Huey, ignoring the signs warning not to cross the runway, and screeched to a halt.

Maria's small army was only metres away from the gate.

Willy jumped down from the cockpit, ducking beneath the whirling blades which whipped the stifling heat into a tornado. His grimy vest had ridden up over his ballooning belly, revealing the tattoo of a naked woman, legs spread open to straddle his hairy belly button. A smouldering cigarette hung out of his parched lips, and he clutched a beer bottle in one hand.

He had fallen a long way from grace in the years since he had left the Vikings, the nickname for Iceland's special forces unit.

Raine grimaced, pushing past Willy as he made an exaggerated display of checking his watch.

"1033," he croaked, shrugging and holding out the palm of his hand. "Deal's a deal, Nate."

An arrow clunked into the metal skin of the helicopter, inches from the Icelander's head. His eyeballs almost rolled out of their sockets as he took in the sight across the other side of the airfield.

"I'll take an IOU," he barked, then ran with more speed than his chunky frame should have been able to handle towards the shelter of the airfield's crumbling tower.

Raine whipped his head around to see what had spooked Willy. His eyes settled on dozens more brightly painted Indians adorned with feathers and bearing bows and blowguns emerging from the line of trees.

Raine hauled himself into the cockpit, projectiles whistling towards him from in front and behind. He powered up the Huey's engines without strapping himself in or making any of the usual checks. The helicopter lifted off the ground, the clatter of impacting stone, wood and metal echoing as it roared forward, over the heads of his attackers and banked out over the ocean of green.

Sighing, Raine relaxed into his seat, fidgeting to get comfortable in nothing but his stolen bathrobe. He pulled a pair of mirrored aviator glasses from a side panel and placed them on his face while shaking his head in amazement.

"I've got some pretty crazy ex-girlfriends," he

said to himself, "but that one is definitely at the top of the list."

Reading his instruments and getting his bearings, he altered the Huey's course, swinging around to the south and glimpsing Willy's airfield below. He guessed at least fifty tribesmen congregated, glaring up at the flying machine, some even loosing arrows in his direction. His eyes fixed on the flash of a white bathrobe within their midst before returning his attention to his destination.

It lay two hours away, but there was no mistaking the ominous presence of Sarisariñama hugging the distant horizon even from this distance.

MARIA tracked the green helicopter as it swung over her head and thundered away to the south, towards its rendezvous with destiny.

She closed her eyes and allowed the sunlight to bathe her face, calming her mind. She ignored the angry protestations of her kin, several of which still fired after the fleeing Huey.

Becoming aware of a presence beside her, she opened her eyes to see Wakondi. Bare chest glistening, the red, yellow and green feathers attached to his headdress denoted him as *a'churi edamo* like her, only far older and wiser. Just like, she realised, any elder should be.

"I have failed," Maria said, hanging her head.

Eyes hard as flint, Wakondi frowned, the clipped language of the Ye'kuana harsh on his tongue. Yet, his words bore no admonishment for her failure.

"You misunderstand your role in the Ye'kuana Promise," he said. "It was not your destiny to stop the Rain King but to guide him." His gaze drifted towards the heavens, light washing over the hard contours of his scarred body.

"The Rain King will unleash the Evil Spirit," Wakondi continued. "It has been foreseen and cannot be changed. But, as is my hope, the guidance you gave him will help steer his hand when the time for him to decide comes."

"But the Rain King is two men," Maria argued.

"Two halves of the same spirit," Wakondi corrected. "And only one shall return from the Dark Mountain. Which one," he concluded, "will determine the fate of all humankind."

NEW ORLEANS USA,

THE wailing had finally ceased.

Unnerving silence settled upon Rudy O'Rourke. Exhaustion crept into every fibre of his being. Still, he summoned the last of his energy reserves to push on, to do what needed to be done.

He turned with as much stealth as he could muster. A floorboard creaked under his weight. He halted his step, raising his foot and making a wider lunge away from the offending floorboard. Silent as a phantom, he made his way through the darkness, down the corridor to his destination. He tried the handle and pushed the door open a jar, wincing at the screech of dry hinges.

Finally, he was through, clicking the door closed behind him.

"Mission accomplished," he whispered. "Target is down."

Zoey glanced at him and smiled. "Good work, soldier," then she patted his side of the bed. "Now, come and finish what we started."

O'Rourke grinned as his wife threw back the covers. He caught a tantalising side view of her body, her smooth black skin reflecting the soft glow of the baby monitor on the nightstand. He glanced at the grainy video, checking that his nine-month-old daughter hadn't tried to out-manoeuvre him again by waking up in the time he took to creep from her room to his. Then he vaulted into bed to continue what he and Zoey had started before the rude interruption.

UNDISCLOSED LOCATION

"WE have a problem."

They were not the words the man in the yellow tie wanted to hear. "Go," he said into the scrambled phone.

On the other end of the line and hundreds of miles away in Baltimore, Jones hesitated. *"The police recovered Braun's phone from the crash."*

"Why is that a problem?"

The pause was longer this time. So long that the man in the yellow tie nearly needed to repeat himself. Luckily for Jones, he didn't.

"We, um . . . We didn't confiscate it when he was with the patient."

Now it was the man in the yellow tie's turn to pause, partly to make Jones sweat, partly to control his anger.

What fucking amateur doesn't confiscate a specialist's personal phone when on a covert op? he thought. He refused to dignify Jones' admission with a response. His silence was enough of a prompt to tease further information from the field agent.

"We've now taken possession of it," Jones explained.

And so revealed our involvement and most likely piqued someone's curiosity, the man in the yellow tie thought, shaking his head and pinching the bridge of his nose.

"It's badly damaged, lots of the data corrupted. But our tech guys managed to retrieve part of an email Braun sent minutes before the crash, just after leaving John Hopkins."

"What did it say?" the man in the yellow tie asked.

"Just four words," Jones replied. *"Did they do it?"* Another pause. Another imminent confession. *"There was an attachment, but the tech guys can't recover enough data to reformat what it contained. They think it was an image file."*

"Who did he send it to?"

"It's a public domain email address for Cornell University in Ithaca. Someone called Henri Moreau. We checked him out. He's a neurotheologist, someone who studies the link between the brain and religious experience-"

"I know what a neurotheologist is," the man in the yellow tie said. He dropped his voice, speaking more to himself than to Jones. "And why Braun sent that email to him."

"What do you want us to-"

"I'll deal with this," the man in the yellow tie cut him off. *And with you and that idiot partner of yours, once this is over,* he thought. "Await further instructions." He hung up and immediately dialled another number. The voice that answered was as crisp and direct as his own. Almost.

"Coe," it said.

"I'm activating you," the man in the yellow tie said. "How soon can you get to Ithaca?"

NEW JERSEY, USA

THE woman who had identified herself only as Coe stepped out of the shower cubicle and towelled herself dry. Stepping into the bedroom, she pulled the towel from her body to rub at her short-cropped hair, stealing a glance in the tall mirror. Her toned, athletic body reflected back, the muscles of her calves and thighs hard, her shoulders broad. She was happy with her body and confident. She no longer lost any sleep over her teenage dream of being more well-endowed on the chest.

She pulled on each item of clothing with precision, neither slowly nor quickly, merely at the optimum speed for such an onerous exercise. Once attired in a trouser suit that was tight enough to highlight her femininity yet loose enough to be practical, she unlocked the top drawer of her bedside cabinet. Nestled within the foam cut-outs of the drawer's lining sat a handgun and two small throwing knives. Donning a holster beneath her suit jacket, she tucked the gun away and slid the knives into sheathes hidden beneath her socks. Then she locked the drawer and repositioned the digital alarm clock she had knocked to return to a perfect viewing angle from her side of the bed.

Taking hold of her prepacked mini suitcase, she headed out of the room and down the corridor. She repositioned the painting of a sun-kissed summer meadow on her way down the stairs. It had been knocked off centre by perhaps two degrees, she guessed.

She arrived in the kitchen twenty seconds before the porch door leading into it burst open.

"Mommy!" Eva shouted. The three-year-old's excitement at seeing her mother was out of proportion for the duration of their separation. She had only been at kindergarten for the morning, yet her joy suggested a separation of several days.

Though she didn't reciprocate her daughter's excitement, she played along. She swept the dark-haired little girl into her arms and gave her an exaggeratedly tight hug.

Her husband followed Eva in, letting a breath of summer heat disrupt the perfect thirty-seven-degree setting of the air conditioning unit. Coe stifled her irritation and generated a perfectly beaming smile on her face as he kissed her.

"All set?" he asked.

"Of course," she replied.

"Oh no, mommy," Eva whined, glancing at the suitcase leaning against the wall. "You're not going away again, are you?"

"Oh, Poppet," Coe replied. "It's just for one night this time. Something tells me this will be an easy job."

Eva was not happy but was accustomed to her mother's absences. "Will you bring me back something?"

"I can't bring you a present every time I go away," Coe replied. Eva's lip dropped into a pout. "But if you're good for Daddy . . ."

"Yay!" Eva cried, hugging her again.

"I've got to go," Coe said. After more unnecessarily elongated displays of affection with her daughter and husband, Coe left the house, placed her suitcase in the car's trunk, and then got in and started the engine. She entered her destination into the sat-nav, shifted into drive and headed off on her mission.

She never gave another thought to her adoring family.

EXTRACT FROM DR BENJAMIN KING'S BLOG:
The Legend of the Moon Mask

AN ancient African legend tells of a day, in deepest, darkest prehistory, when a piece of the moon fell from the sky.

A simple man found it; some say he was a goat-herd, some say he was a blacksmith, and one account even says he was a slave.

Whoever this man was, he fashioned the fallen piece of the moon into a beautiful mask, and when he wore it, it showed him events before they happened.

Many versions of this 'Moon Mask' story are known across the African continent. In some, the man uses the mask to manipulate others and amass great wealth. In others, he uses it to accumulate power and authority. In some, the legend even says he used the mask to travel through time. He manipulated the future or changed the past so that, rather than growing up a goat-herd, blacksmith or slave, he became a great king, ruling over a vast kingdom.

Whatever the details, the overall theme of this story remains the same across the different cultures that have retained it. The Moon Mask was so powerful that it corrupted even the most innocent men.

Fearing it, the gods themselves intervened.

They shattered the mask into several pieces and scattered it across the earth so that no mortal could again command its extraordinary ability.

I first heard of this myth as a young boy, travelling with my father through the Gambia in West Africa.

I spent time in Nigeria as a toddler. But I had been too young to remember much beyond the terrifying day that I witnessed the murder of my mother and sister. Africa had, therefore, become a dark place for me, a land haunted by ghosts and monsters.

I had no desire to return.

When I was eight, however, my father

made/forced/cajoled/practically-kidnapped me to accompany him on a trip to The Gambia. My sister and I were the first of the King family to have been born outside Africa. In the fallout of the Lagos tragedy, he felt it was vital for me to see our family's ancestral home.

On our second week in the country, we made an uncomfortable, six-hour journey deep inland to the village of Wassu. On the outskirts of the village, I came face-to-face with the first of the eleven stone circles that litter the area.

And a secret that would redirect the course of my life.

Even now, locals insist a curse will fall upon anyone who disturbs the remains of the ancient kings they believe lie entombed beneath the stone circles. They place small stones and vegetables upon the pillars, perhaps as an offering to the ancients, perhaps as a way of appeasing the curse . . . no one knows.

I wandered around the ruins, entranced by their beauty, listening to the rhythmic drumming of an entrepreneurial musician (who, of course, wanted a few *dalasi* as payment).

But I found myself drawn to one particular tale my father told me.

A sequel to the 'Legend of the Moon Mask,' I suppose you could say; folklore retained by only a handful of people who claim descent from the mythical Bouda tribe.

A story about what happened after the ancient gods had cast the mask asunder.

In a tale sharing remarkable similarities with Moses and his burning bush, Al'I'Dum, a member of a persecuted lower caste, sought shelter from his masters. He hid within the Wassu Stone Circles, and it was here that he encountered one of the Old Gods.

It appeared to him in the form of a hyena. It told him to lead his people, the Bouda, the Children of the Gods, to freedom and seek shelter in their ancestral City of the Moon, at the foot of the Lunar Mountain.

The hyena gave Al'I'Dum a single, broken piece of the original Moon Mask. It granted him glimpses of the future.

(I know this contradicts the story of the Old Gods removing the mask from human temptation, but such is the way with ancient mythology).

Anyway, so armed, Al'I'Dum prepared his people for their exodus, waiting for a day he had foreseen when their masters' attention turned towards an invading foreign king.

Disguising themselves as hyenas, the Bouda escaped their masters and journeyed deep into the heart of Africa. Their adventures across the wilderness parallel many similar odysseys. They encounter monsters and savage cannibals, dodge erupting volcanoes, navigate raging rivers, etcetera, etcetera.

But, after undoubtedly embellished trials and tribulations, the Bouda arrived at the City of the Moon, built long ago by the Old Gods. And, there, at the foot of the Lunar Mountain, they remained for countless generations, protected by their *oni,* their Great King, who fashioned the piece of the Moon Mask into a new façade. For he was the only one who could resist the mask's power, its curse, and use it for good, to foresee dangers that the Bouda faced and protect them from the world's evils.

But, eventually, the mask and the king failed them, and a great doom fell upon the people of the Lunar Mountain.

"The Moon Mask is real," I remember my father saying as we stood within the stone circle.

The rhythmic beat of the entrepreneurial drummer echoed into the dusty, blood-red sunset as my young mind absorbed the great fantasy of what my father was telling me.

Was it even possible?

While magical masks, hyena-gods and time travel were obviously the result of centuries of poetic embellishment, my imagination couldn't help but dream.

Did some truth lie at the heart of the Legend of the Moon Mask?

My father's next words stripped away any such dream and wrenched me back into a nightmare I had tried to forget.

"It is what your mum and sister died for."

12:

UNESCO BASE CAMP, SARISARIÑAMA TEPUI, VENEZUELA

"A storm is coming," Professor Juliet McKinney announced, the canvas sides of the medical tent slapping, caught by a sudden gust. If King didn't know any better, he would have thought the Scottish woman had choreographed it for dramatic emphasis.

"We must move fast," she continued. "That chamber has been protected for god-only-knows-how-long. But now there's a gaping hole in its ceiling it could fill with water when the tunnels flood, destroying whatever archaeology hasn't already been lost."

Though she kept her attention fixed on Nadia, King knew she directed the last comment at him.

It had been three hours since his literal escape from the jaws of death. He, Sid and Nadia had spent much of that time on the end of Professor McKinney's scathing reprimand. She had given little consideration to King's injury, or the concussion Nadia had diagnosed him with as the expedition's chief first-aider. Instead, she had stood in the cramped tent, barking at them about their inexcusable breach of protocol by not reporting the discovery of the hidden tunnel to her.

"You endangered your lives and the lives of the rescue team I'd have to have sent if you all had fallen into that chamber," she had snapped, ninety-nine per cent of her ire targeted at King.

"Not to mention the destruction you have wrought upon the archaeology by your piss-poor mishandling of the site," she'd continued. "You've disturbed the original archaeological context, making no recording of it. You've removed objects from their primary context. You've handled sensitive organic materials without gloves, contaminating them with dirt and oils from your skin.

"I shouldn't have to be telling you this! It's the sort of behaviour you wouldn't accept from a first-year undergrad on one of your own digs. I bloody well won't accept it on mine, especially not from someone holding a doctorate!"

King could not argue with the Scot's point any more than he could explain his compulsion to retrieve the mask. Yet, while he had admitted his accountability, the expedition leader insisted on raising it again at any opportunity.

This time, however, King had a response prepared. "I think the chamber fills with water whenever the tunnels flood," he said. "There are drains in the ceiling and floor level, and what I think is a 'high-tide' mark on the wall."

McKinney sighed, flicking her wild mane of auburn hair out of her eyes and planting her hands on her hips. While her physical lifestyle kept her body trim, her clothing was more appropriate for a woman twenty years younger. A tight pair of shorts, no longer than hot pants, revealed the weathered, leather-like skin of long, freckled legs. A loose khaki vest-top highlighted her disinterest in wearing a bra.

"I've not got time to listen to your 'fancy sewer' theory again," she groaned, cutting off his response and re-directing her attention to Nadia. "Be ready to move the moment Nate gets here," she ordered, turning on her heel to march out of the tent.

"Nate?" King repeated. "As in . . . Nathan Raine? What's he got to do with anything?"

"Mister Raine has a background in search and rescue," McKinney replied, halting just inside the tent flap but obscuring the mountaintop view beyond. "He'll be going down with the team to help retrieve the skeleton."

While the chamber and tunnels were littered with human remains, there was no way of retrieving them before the storm hit. However, the skeleton he had found with the mask, sword, and dagger was a potential anomaly that needed retrieving and protecting as quickly as possible.

"I don't need Raine on my team," King said, failing to hide the disdain in his tone. "He's nothing but a washed-up, low-life jack-of-all-trades. He certainly isn't qualified to record an archaeological context."

"Based on your slap-dash handling of the site, neither are you," McKinney shot back. "And, despite your newfound Crocodile Dundee credentials, even you are not qualified to retrieve archaeological material from a crocodile-infested underground chamber."

King probed the large gash on his head, sealed with paper stitches. "I'm fine," he said, resisting the urge to massage his temples to relieve the persistent throbbing behind his eyes.

But McKinney wasn't concerned about his physical welfare. "You're far from it, laddie," she snarled. "You're clearly not thinking straight, acting rashly, impulsively. I don't know what got into you down in those tunnels today, but you're not going anywhere near them again until I say so."

"What?" King erupted, but the Scot had already pushed through the tent flaps and into the sunshine. King raced after her.

"Ben, no," Sid called to his back.

King stalked after the expedition leader, ignoring the activity of the base camp as researchers returned from the tunnels for an extended lunch break.

Nestled between the yawning expanse of the table mountain's largest sinkhole, *Sima Humboldt*, and its sheer cliffs, the camp was a sprawling canvas city. The largest tents ringed the perimeter, encircling the array of fifty-or-so two-person units that formed the main sleeping area. Beyond them lay the shower and toilet facilities, while off to one side sat del Vega's mini sub-camp.

Raphael del Vega was in charge of the contingent of Venezuelan Bolivarian Militiamen which the expedition's host country had insisted accompany the scientists – supposedly for their protection, though King suspected it was more to keep an eye on what UNESCO was up to in their territory.

"Hey Ben," Yosef greeted him with a smile. "Is it true? Did you find something down there?"

The Israeli archaeologist's words couldn't penetrate King's seething rage as he grasped his boss by the shoulder and whirled her around to face him.

"How dare-"

"You're sending that unqualified, arrogant American knob to recover my find and leaving me up here?" King demanded.

McKinney's face burned, her eyes darkening with anger. "I'm sending a team of the most qualified people on this dig to sort out your fuck up," she replied. "Raine's background makes him the perfect person to take the lead in such a delicate operation. Nadia will be there to ensure everything is handled according to best archaeological practices. Del Vega and his men will take care of your little crocodile infestation."

"While the documentary cameras focus on our illustrious leader, no doubt?"

Yosef grimaced and took an exaggerated step back, exchanging a glance with Sid and Nadia as they caught up with King. The wind blew their hair around their faces but did little to ease the sweltering heat as the sun beat down on the camp, unobstructed by the clouds hanging below the summit.

However, there was a single, red-headed cloud

on the summit, and it darkened before the eyes of the gathering crowd.

"Do you really expect us to give up the chance to boost our viewership numbers?" McKinney demanded. "Sharpe Enterprises and The Adventure Channel are this expedition's biggest commercial sponsors, investing millions in return for exclusive footage. All we've given them so far is a new species of butterfly. But this discovery is more exciting than anyone expected. Done right, it could put us smack bang back in the spotlight and secure our funding to continue what we've started here."

"And you're obviously the one to be in the limelight," King scoffed.

"I am the expedition leader."

"And I know more about what's down there than anyone."

McKinney let out a bitter cackle. "You stumbled upon it, King! You fell through a hole in the floor. It could have happened to anyone. That hardly makes you an expert."

"I know who that skeleton is."

"Oh really?" McKinney scoffed. "Because identifying a single individual in the archaeological record is that easy?"

"It is if you know what to look for: a tricorn, a matching gold sword and dagger . . . and a magical mask."

McKinney rolled her eyes, turning away.

"It's the Black Death," King shouted after her.

"What's the plague got to do with anything?" Yosef mumbled.

"Not the plague," King snapped, keeping his attention on McKinney. "The pirate."

"The pirate?" McKinney turned back, her face incredulous.

"Between 1728 and 1736, scattered reports about a pirate, known only as the Black Death, circulated the Caribbean."

"I know the story," McKinney said. "A Caribbean folktale about an escaped African slave, raiding plantations and slave ships to free others from captivity."

"That's right," King pressed. "To the modern-day descendants of the black Caribbean slaves, he's kind of like a King Arthur or a Robin Hood character - little more than a legend. He's described as a giant of a man, wielding a matching golden sword and dagger. He brought death and terror to the slave masters but offered hope to those he saved, giving them a new life aboard his ship, the *Hand of Freedom*."

"Like you said: a legend."

"But he was more than a legend," King continued. "Just like King Arthur was most likely based on a 5th Century warlord. He didn't have a magical sword, a kingdom called Camelot or his Knights of the Round Table, but there was a person whose legacy extended beyond death. Whose story was built up until he became something bigger, something greater than a mere mortal: a hero."

McKinney eyed him, her forehead creasing into a frown as though struggling to remember something. For a moment, it appeared she might hear him out, but then the memory surfaced.

"I've read your doctoral thesis, King," she said, shaking her head in exasperation. "I remember the strand of evidence you tried to apply to you and your father's ridiculous Progenitor Theory. I am not prepared to stand here arguing about it now."

McKinney spun and marched away through the canvas city.

"What sort of scientist does that make you?" King shouted after her. "What sort of scientist refuses to entertain alternative points of view? What sort of example does that set to this team, huh? That it's your way or the highway?"

A larger crowd had gathered to see what the commotion was about. Dirt-smeared archaeologists and other personnel gawped at the arguing pair. Sid and Nadia hung back, unsure when to intervene, watching as McKinney stopped next to one of the camp's large solar panels. But as she turned to face King, conscious of the expectant faces surrounding her, her expression was anything but sunny.

King had backed her into a corner, and everyone knew it.

"You know what, King? It's been a stressful couple of hours. I could use some light entertainment. So, tell us," she said, throwing open her arms to encompass the crowd. "Tell us about your pirates and your magical time-travelling mask. That is what your mother and sister died for, isn't it?"

"It is what your mum and sister died for."

His father's voice echoed in King's mind, and, for a moment, the vivid memory consumed King. It was as though he sat around that campfire in Wassu with his father again. The setting sun's rays warmed his face; the sound of chirping insects replaced the drummer's monotonous beat.

"The Moon Mask is real. It is what your mum and sister died for."

At the time of Abuku's attack on the King's rented apartment in Lagos, the Moon Mask, the Bouda, and the Progenitors were nothing more than collected folktales. Reginald King had only started unifying these threads into an archaeological theory. He had spent two months in Nigeria investigating possible links between the Yoruba people and the mythological Bouda. His family had flown over to spend Ramadan with him.

No one had predicted the political turmoil that arose, exploding in hours into a full-blown military coup. It was fuelled by ethnic violence and driven by General Abago Abuku's continent-spanning regime of ethnic cleansing.

'Africa for Africans,' was his motto. Many flocked to his bloody cause: those disillusioned by the meddling of foreign powers in national affairs, or the wealth amassed by non-Africans on their blood, sweat and sacrifice.

Reginald's focus on African cultural origins turned the genocidal madman's attention towards the King family. He had terrorised, raped and murdered them before his eyes, all to get his hands on the one symbol he believed would unify Africa: the Moon Mask.

"What better symbol exists to unite the disparate countries and peoples of an entire continent?" King's father had recited around the campfire. *"It is the evidence that people, who many Western societies viewed as primitive, had built the world's first civilisation and spread it across the globe."*

But, at that point, the evidence Abuku sought did not exist. No matter how hard he tried to convince his family's captors of this, Reginald King could not save them. He barely escaped with his terrorised son and his own life.

From that day on, Reginald's academic theory had mutated into a personal obsession, a desperate attempt to prove that his family hadn't been butchered for nothing.

Within the magical stone circles of Wassu, Little Benny, too, had slipped into his father's quest. Growing into adulthood, he and his father had fleshed out the Bouda and the Progenitors, joined ancient dots into a vaguely discernible picture revealing the cultural origins of humankind.

What they lacked was the ability to test their hypothesis against hard, concrete evidence.

Until now.

"It is what your mum and sister died for."

His father's words echoed through his mind, sending a bolt of electric fire dancing across the back of King's eyes. He pounded his eye sockets with the balls of both palms as though the pressure would relieve the agony. But, like some fanged creature squirming through the tissue of his brain, a new memory chewed to the surface. His father stood before him for a second, as solid and as real as the gawping crowd.

"They weren't the first," he continued, simultaneously standing on the summit of Sarisariñama and sitting around the campfire at Wassu.

"And they won't be the last."

13:

NEW ORLEANS, USA,

THE crack of wrenching rock thundered in his ears. Thick plumes of dust choked him, clogging his nostrils and mixing with saliva to paint his throat in a suffocating cement. Flashes of light assaulted his eyes, muzzle-flash searing his retinas. The hammer of machine-gun fire blended with the orchestra of his teammates' death cries.

Then the weight of the earth above the tunnel crashed down upon him. He fell to the ground but even his panicked thrashing could not save him from being buried alive.

The last thing he saw before darkness entombed him was the devil standing at the far end of the corridor. Blue, ice-cold eyes flashed in his direction-

"You're up early, baby."

O'Rourke spun around, lunging for the speaker.

Zoey screamed, darting backwards, instinctively turning Lyla away from him, shielding her baby.

Their baby.

"Zoey," O'Rourke gasped. Then his eyes settled on the knife in his hand, the terror in his wife's eyes. He'd used it to dice bacon before throwing it into the pan of eggs scrambling on the hob. Now he stared at it in horror, dropping it as though it scorched his palm.

"I'm sorry," he said. "I'm so sorry. I was just dicing the-"

"It's okay," Zoey said, sliding Lyla into her highchair sat next to the breakfast island in the middle of the kitchen. Early morning sunlight streamed across their backyard and in through the windows. "It's okay," she said again, stepping towards him.

Despite her words, O'Rourke sensed the caution she displayed. Her eyes were locked on him, and he was sure he felt his heart break some more at the glint of fear in them. However, despite that fear, she bent down to retrieve the knife and placed it safely on the worktop. Then she drew him into a gentle kiss.

"No harm done," she whispered.

"This time," he replied, eyes downcast.

"I shouldn't have snuck up on you," Zoey said. "I heard you shouting out again in the night . . . calling his name. I know you're always on edge after the nightmare. Let's just forget it, yeah? We had such a nice time last night, despite interruptions-" as if on cue, Lyla made a laughing noise from across the kitchen. "I'd hate to ruin the weekend."

O'Rourke opened his mouth to say something further, but it wasn't his voice that came out.

"Eggs? Awesome!"

Petey bulldozed into the kitchen, his Spider-Man dressing gown swirling around him like a cape. He flew into his father's arms, the big man picking him up and whirling him around.

"Hey, Sport," O'Rourke said, giving the five-year-old a bear hug. Then, still in his arms, Petey leaned over to kiss Zoey.

"Love you, Mommy," he said. "Daddy's cooking eggs."

"I can see."

"Oh man," O'Rourke said. "Did you want eggs? I only made enough for me, Mommy and Ly."

"Oh, Daddy! You're joking." Then the little

boy's face turned serious. "You *are* joking, aren't you?"

O'Rourke kept his expression serious for a heartbeat longer, then smiled. Petey's own grin was almost identical.

People often marvelled at the similarity between them. Lyla had her mom's delicate beauty. On the other hand, Petey had inherited his father's robust features, from his squared jawline and broad nose to his wide brown eyes and midnight skin. But it was the beaming smile that was the most distinctive feature of the O'Rourke men.

Laughing, O'Rourke returned to preparing breakfast, forgetting what had happened - or nearly happened - and pushing aside the nightmares that assaulted him as much during the day as at night.

At least for the moment.

His grandfather had always said that, whatever else happened in the day, a family should always start it with a hearty breakfast and a hearty laugh. It was a sentiment O'Rourke kept with him, and their morning meals were usually light and happy affairs.

He laid out the spread of eggs, scrambled with onions, tomato and bacon, French toast, orange juice and steaming coffee for him and Zoey.

For a moment, he dared think that it was too happy. Too good. Even when the doorbell rang and Zoey went to answer it with a smile on her face, he dared to imagine this morning routine lasting for every day of his life.

That was until Zoey, smile replaced by a frown, returned.

Lawrence Gibbs followed her into the kitchen, and, just like that, O'Rourke felt that moment of morning bliss evaporate.

"Uncle Laurie!" Petey exclaimed, diving from his chair and hugging the newcomer. Gibbs was not a child-friendly kind of guy, but he had always made an effort with O'Rourke's son. O'Rourke enjoyed the look of discomfort on Gibbs' acne-scarred face but appreciated his attempt at a smile. Lyla, however, her face smeared with egg, snot and tomato sauce, received little more than a disgusted glance before Gibbs turned his attention to him.

"Got a sec?"

O'Rourke's heart sank, knowing Gibbs' words meant only one thing: something bad was about to happen.

Really bad.

14:

JAMAICA, 1727

"WE propagate it from cuttings, you see," the well-spoken gentleman continued. "Some plantations still grow the cane from seeds, your father's included. But that is a rather outdated method now. You see, after each harvest, the cane sends up new stalks which we call ratoons-"

"But *why* do you set fire to the field?" Jessica asked again.

Emily Hamilton rolled her eyes. Her friend had asked the same question some minutes ago. Instead of giving her a straight answer, Charles Banks had decided to explain the entire propagating, planting, and harvesting of the sugar crop process from scratch.

I've lived on a plantation like this all my life, she thought. *I think I know more about sugar than some self-righteous naval officer who has inherited his family business and is trying to convince my father to sell me to him. I mean to marry him*, she amended in her head.

For a moment, she fancied she was little more than one of the Negro slaves working the fields around her. Then she banished such a notion. Her sufferings were nothing compared to the poor souls her father, Banks, and his ilk considered their property.

Judging by how tightly he's gripping my arm, Banks already thinks he owns me too.

"Well, it's quite simple, dear Jessica," Banks answered. "It is to burn away any dry leaves and, most importantly, kill any venomous snakes hiding in the grass. After all, these slaves are quite an investment."

Jessica and Francesca, the second leach desperately trying to grasp onto the lieutenant commander, burst into laughter. Hysterical laughter that was unwarranted for even the funniest joke, let alone one lacking any humour whatsoever. Indeed, Banks' puzzled look indicated the conviction behind his words. He wasn't trying to be humorous, just stating a fact.

Emily glared at her three companions before turning her gaze to the young black maid sweltering in the midday sun while holding a frilly parasol over their heads.

Hopefully, she doesn't understand his words, she thought, knowing many of her father's workers had yet to learn English. But the moisture in the girl's eyes as she tilted her head to the ground suggested otherwise.

As they continued their forced march around the plantation, Emily tried to pull further away from Banks. Banks, in return, gripped her arm more tightly in the crook of his elbow. Whatever spell he held over Jessica and Francesca seemed to work in reverse on her. His handsome features seemed boyish, his expensive attire unsightly. Even his voice irritated her, having descended from a dull monotone to unadulterated arrogance.

And father actually expects me to fall head over heels with this man after one walk around the plantation?

She knew, however, that love did not factor into her father's equations.

Their path led them around the edge of a vast sugar cane field, the largest on the island. The area was a hive of activity as the black African workers controlled a line of fire, blazing from one side of the crop to the other. In the fire's wake, a whole army of workers slashed and hacked at the standing cane, leaving the stalks just above ground level. Behind them came more workers who collected the harvested cane in wicker baskets. Most were children, but a few were older women.

"But why doesn't the sugar cane burn?" Francesca pressed.

"Because sugar cane stalks and roots are rich in water content and so resist the flames," Emily snapped before she could stop herself. The two women stared at her, seemingly mortified that a young woman should know such details. Banks tried but failed to mask his irritation at her interruption.

She ignored them all, focusing instead on the field. She could feel the heat of the fire washing over her, but the absence of wind drove the smoke into a vertical funnel cutting into the sapphire sky.

All around the fire, black workers stood ready with buckets of water. They threw their contents down to direct the flames and prevent them from getting out of control. Ahead of the fire, a small group of the workers sat on the ground, scrambling for whatever shade they could find whilst enjoying a brief rest from their labours.

Then something caught her eye.

"That man," she said to Banks, pointing across the field to a figure sitting apart. Even seated beneath the boughs of a palm tree, she noticed the enormity of his frame. Easily twice the girth of an average man and a head taller. "Why does he sit alone?"

On her father's plantation, she had noticed that the enslaved workers usually exhibited a great sense of community. Even here on the Banks plantation, her father's biggest rivals, she hadn't seen a single black man, woman or child alone. A by-product, she supposed, of the horrendous hand fate had dealt them.

Banks followed her gaze, his face twisting into a look of even greater contempt than he usually exhibited towards his slaves.

"They say he's cursed," Banks explained. "The only survivor of the *L'aille Raptor*."

"The *L'aille Raptor*?" Jessica and Francesca repeated in unison.

Emily knew the story, of course. In the two years since a Jamaica-based Royal Navy vessel had found the slave ship adrift near the island, the *Raptor* had become something of a horror story. They said the captain had gone mad, and the crew transformed into hideous monsters. Some tales supposed the ship had been dragged into, then escaped from, Davy Jones' Locker, the sailors' hell. Others said they had resorted to cannibalism. But the *Raptor's* fate was more often attributed to a heathen curse. Even the rescue team from the navy ship had supposedly succumbed to the voodoo magic.

"Quite the bargain, really," Banks continued, his standard arrogance masking any unease he felt about the curse. "A slave of his size and strength should have cost me five times what I paid for him. But nobody else wanted him. Too terrified of the curse," he scoffed. "Some even call him 'the Black Death.'" He laughed, shaking his head. "Load of superstitious nonsense if you ask me."

"You don't believe in the curse?" Francesca asked, eyes wide.

"What sort of god-fearing man would believe such savage mumbo jumbo?"

But Emily tuned out of Banks' diatribe as they continued across the field, steering clear of the wall of flame. Instead, she focussed on the enormous African. His head lolled back against the tree trunk, eyes closed. As they got nearer, Emily noted the puckered flesh on the midnight skin of his bare chest. Scars, she realised, sickened as she imagined what horrors he had endured.

Then, as though sensing her interest, the African's eyes snapped open, locking onto hers. Emily's heart raced faster, mesmerised by the intensity of the man's gaze.

What wonders have those eyes seen? she mused. *What adventures has he been on in his native land?*

She pictured the exotic beauty of Africa from snippets she'd seen in books. Too often, she had overheard her father's acquaintances describe it as a godforsaken land. It was populated by cannibals and savages, teeming with snakes and beasts, beset by fiery volcanoes and torn apart by raging waterfalls. But, in her mind's eye, she saw a world of outstanding beauty: rivers flowed from lush mountains, through tropical forests and into grasslands teeming with wildlife of the most glorious kind. And the people, those so-called savages and cannibals? She had seen them gathered in the slave barracks at the end of the working day, forcing song, dance, and even laughter through the misery fate had dealt them. Even in the eyes of the most resentful slave, she had seen nothing but a well of anguish and pain rather than evil.

They are as human as the rest of us, she decided, *and need to be treated thus.* Yet, she had never encountered another white person who shared such a mentality.

Feeling somehow excited and vulnerable under the big man's intense gaze, Emily broke contact, forcing herself to tune back into Banks' mundane diatribe.

A loud creaking assaulted her ears at the exact moment the ground seemed to depress beneath her weight. Then, with the tortured wrenching of rotten wood, the floor imploded, swallowing her. She felt Banks scramble to retain his lock on her arm but failed. Jessica, Francesca and the maid dived away from the ever-widening hole in the ground.

Emily dropped, her stomach lurching, her body twisting. Wood, stone and lumps of earth bounced and crashed off each other, enveloping her in a choking cloud.

She hit the ground hard, screaming at the jolt of agony from her left ankle as it crunched beneath her weight. Piles of soil and shattered lengths of timbre crushed her, pinning her to the bottom of the hole, suffocating her cry for help as darkness claimed her.

15:

UNESCO BASE CAMP, SARISARIÑAMA TEPUI, VENEZUELA

"**BEN?**" Sid asked, taking her boyfriend's arm as he pummelled his eyes with the balls of his hands.

"I said you should rest," Nadia said, stepping to King's other side, her face a mixture of concern and irritation.

"I'm okay," King waved them off. "It's just a headache."

Sid watched her boyfriend recompose himself. But, while he hid the pain, he could not conceal the twitch of emotion on his face. By mentioning his mother and sister, McKinney had touched a far more sensitive nerve than his concussion.

Sid felt a surge of fury pulsate through her. Fury at McKinney for throwing King's ambush back on him, herself for not intervening, and King for his arrogance, thinking he could take on a conniving personality like the professor in front of an audience and come out on top.

The Sarisariñama Expedition was meant to be a new start for her and King. But it seemed the Black Death was destined to haunt them as much as the ghosts of her boyfriend's family.

"Okay." King rose to McKinney's challenge, and Sid knew it took all his self-control not to respond to her quip about his family tragedy.

"Ben," she whispered. "You don't have to do this."

She knew how much her boyfriend hated talking before large audiences and how most audiences responded to some of his less conventional ideas. Marc Duval, King's former professor and his father's best friend, had forced his inclusion on the expedition upon McKinney on the agreement he left his Progenitor Theory behind.

Now, it seemed, King had walked into a trap of his own making, breaking that agreement and opening himself to ridicule.

He glanced at the eager faces of the crowd

gathering around the tents. The reddening of the circular scar on his forehead betrayed his embarrassment.

"The Caribbean legend of the Black Death is more than some folk tale," he began, ignoring Sid's advice and adopting his university lecturer tone. "Two references support the oral traditions. The first is the log entry of a Spanish treasure galleon. The *San Jose* reported being attacked off the coast of modern-day Florida and boarded by a ship crewed by escaped slaves. The ship's colours bore the shape of a hand – the 'Hand of Freedom' - and her captain was a 'giant, black man wielding a matching gold sword and dagger'."

"And the second?" McKinney didn't bother to hide her impatience.

"A letter written by a Jesuit missionary based on the southern tip of what would become French Indochina, dated April 6, 1734. Alexandre de Rhodes petitioned the French government to intervene to secure developing trade interests in the Gulf of Siam. In an example of the lawlessness he had witnessed, he described frequent attacks on settlements and ships by a pirate matching the Black Death's description."

"Siam?" McKinney scoffed. "Rather a long way from Florida and the Caribbean, wouldn't you say? Why sail all the way to modern-day Thailand to plunder ships and find buried treasure?" McKinney asked. A laughable attempt at a pirate accent highlighted the cliché.

"The Black Death wasn't interested in treasure."

"No," McKinney agreed. "He was the self-less Zorro-like hero of the New World."

"No," King cut her off. "The consequences of his actions led to hyperbole about his motives - it may have even fuelled the First Maroon War. But he didn't intend to trigger a slave revolution or be hailed a hero. He was just a man . . . a man searching for a specific prize."

Sid grimaced, sensing the noose tightening around King's neck.

"The Moon Mask," his redheaded wannabe-executioner grinned as though she had just won the argument. She turned to face the crowd, spreading her arms as if to embrace them, play-acting as a lawyer making her final speech to the Bench.

"And there we have it," McKinney said, sunlight bringing out the freckles on her cheeks even as the wind whipped her wild mane around her shoulders. "The inevitable Holy Grail of Doctor King's research, the answer to any question you throw at him. What was the Black Death searching for? The magical, time-travelling Moon Mask, of course. What is the evidence for the origins of civilisation? The Moon Mask. Who built the pyramids? Where do babies come from? Who shot J.R.? The Moon Mask, the Moon Mask, the Moon Mask!"

The audience laughed, and Sid felt her cheeks flush, sensing King's humiliation. His response, however, was more violent, his limbs quaking with barely suppressed rage.

"Easy," she whispered, taking his hand while glaring at her boss. While Sid hated the Moon Mask and King's obsession with it more than anyone, McKinney's taunts were cruel. The academic community had derided King and his father for daring to propose something outside the box.

The physical contact calmed King; it was the first time Sid had felt important to him in many months.

He took a deep breath and then continued.

"I believe the Black Death scoured the earth," he said, stepping closer to the crowd as though beseeching his colleagues personally. "He travelled any distance necessary, searching for all the pieces of the original Moon Mask so he could claim its power. I am not saying," he added, glaring at the smirking faces, "I believe in the mask's magical properties. I am saying that the Black Death and his people did."

"His people?" McKinney repeated, realisation

dawning. "You think he was part of the Bouda Tribe, don't you? Even though they're just as much a myth as the Black Death."

"The Bouda are a real people," Sid snapped. "They're an ethnic minority living near Wassu in The Gambia."

"I know that," McKinney replied. "But their claim to have descended from a great civilisation of warriors that could turn into hyenas is preposterous."

"While researching the origins of the Bouda," King cut in, forcing professionalism into his voice, "my father and I spent several months travelling with a group of Tuareg nomads around the Sahara. One of their stories tells of how, several hundred years ago, one of their parties fled a violent enemy. They sought shelter in a great stone city: the fabled City of the Moon. There, a prince named Kha'um fought and destroyed the Tuareg's enemies and offered them sanctuary. As thanks, they gave him a sword and a dagger."

McKinney shook her head, letting out a derisive snort. "Let me guess: made of gold?"

"Not gold," King corrected. "Brass . . . which, in the heat of battle, could be mistaken for gold."

There were several murmurs of ascent and nodding heads, but McKinney's continued to shake. She began to pace, not bothering to hide her frustration, flitting in and out of what little shade the trees surrounding the camp offered from the midday sun.

"Graffiti on one of the standing stones at Wassu," King continued, "depicts a black-hulled ship coming to a great stone city. Its inhabitants are loaded onboard in chains. The figure of a man is almost buried beneath overlapping images depicting men, women and children being herded like cattle onto a European ship. He wears a brightly coloured mask and holds what one could interpret as a golden sword and dagger.

"Additionally, the modern-day Bouda are a tiny tribe in the eastern Gambia. They have a rich oral tradition. They claim to be the descendants of the survivors of a great civilisation that was enslaved by 'white devils'."

"Hardly an earth-shattering conclusion, given that twelve million Africans entered the Atlantic slave trade at its height."

"You don't need to lecture me about the slave trade," King growled, hackles rising at the Scottish woman's flippant remark. McKinney backed into the crowd, King's eyes tracking her, burning with dark fury.

"In 1725," he forced the words out of his mouth, "a Lieutenant Percival Lowe of the HMS

Swallow made a log entry. He had boarded the slave ship *L'aille Raptor,* found drifting off the coast of Jamaica. Onboard, he found all but one of the human cargo had died of starvation because all the crew, except the captain, had died of disease. He found the captain, an Englishman named Edward Pryce, horribly disfigured, cradling a brightly coloured mask and rocking back and forth like a madman."

"And you think the surviving slave," McKinney realised, "this Kha'um, King of the Bouda, became the Black Death?"

"I'm certain," King replied. "After gaining his freedom, he scoured the earth, searching for all the pieces of the original Moon Mask. He believed he could reunite them and claim control over time itself."

"So he could travel back in time and save his people from near-extinction?"

"Exactly."

Sid knew the story well. She had spent hours helping her boyfriend cross-reference the possible sightings of the Black Death with so-called Moon Mask myths from around the world. She had helped tie them into a narrative that coincided with the *L'aille Raptor's* transatlantic crossing and the dating of the Wassu graffiti.

But they had never found any undisputable correlation and, therefore, any support within the academic community. Pursuing the Black Death and the Moon Mask had almost cost King his career. He clung to a smidgen of professional respect by the skin of his teeth, and Sid knew that was why Duval had orchestrated his place on Sarisariñama. To hide him away from his critics.

"But now," McKinney said, eyes narrowing. She tried but failed to completely hide the smirk that turned the corners of her lips up. "Now you've added a new chapter to your farcical tale."

And with her words, Sid sensed the trapdoor beneath King's feet spring open, and the noose snap around her boyfriend's neck.

Juliet McKinney, one his most outspoken critics, had him exactly where she wanted him.

16:

NEW ORLEANS USA,

O'ROURKE hesitated, sensing Zoey's frustrated glare. He caught her eye, offering an unspoken apology for Gibbs' intrusion into their family time.

"Come on, Petey, teeth time," she said, plucking Lyla from her highchair.

"Oh, but I want to see Uncle-"

"Now," Zoey snapped, but O'Rourke knew her son wasn't the target of her ire. With the reluctance of a man marching to the gallows, Petey followed his mom out of the kitchen and up the stairs.

O'Rourke glanced at Gibbs. A heartbeat

passed, and then he took a deep breath and rose from his chair. "Coffee?" he asked.

"No. Thank you," Gibbs added. When it came to manners, O'Rourke's superior often reminded him of his son: in need of prompting.

Pouring himself another cup from the simmering pot, he gestured for Gibbs to follow him outside. He guessed that whatever his boss had to say was probably classified or at least sensitive. Even upstairs, Zoey might overhear.

"Watch out for booby traps," he joked, just as Gibbs tripped on the edge of a toddler's seesaw shaped like a caterpillar and let out a curse.

Safely away from discarded children's toys, the two men sat on a swing seat overlooking the lawn. The occasional car droned along the road on the other side of the garden fence.

"So, how you doing?" Gibbs asked. He hid his Texan twang as a matter of habit, knowing the tell-tale drawl was an unwanted distinguishing feature in the field. In their line of work, the fewer distinctive features, the better.

"The doctor says you're fit for duty. Physically, anyway," he added, locking his dark eyes on O'Rourke.

O'Rourke didn't meet his gaze but looked

across the garden and took a sip of his coffee. He relished the kiss of sunlight against his black skin. Gibbs, however, sought the shade of the seat's canopy.

"I'm doing alright," O'Rourke lied. "But there's something I've been meaning to tell you."

Gibbs said nothing but did not avert his gaze.

Damn, does the man even have irises? he wondered. The dark orbs of Gibbs' eyes seemed like intense pools of inky blackness. They still unnerved him, even after so many years.

He drew in a deep breath, then let it out again. "I'm done," he said.

"Done?" Gibbs repeated.

"I can't do it anymore, Boss," O'Rourke explained. The term 'Boss' was an unofficial title, denoting Gibbs' position as team leader. Technically, when one joined their Special Operations team, the previous concept of rank became irrelevant. They were simply operators. Numbers. But, somewhere way back in their unit's covert history, 'Boss' had come into use. And it had stuck.

"This is because of that kid?" Gibbs asked.

O'Rourke closed his eyes, a flash of that terrible moment replaying itself again.

"Do you ever think about Kongessa?"

Gibbs snapped his head away as though O'Rourke had just slapped him. "What's that got to do-"

"I've been having nightmares about it. Again," O'Rourke admitted. "About what . . ." he hesitated, the name on his tongue. Gibbs' new glare challenged him to say it. "About what *he* did."

"You should have nightmares after what that piece of shit did to us."

"But what if . . . what if-"

"Don't say it," Gibbs growled. "Don't even think it, not for a moment. What he did was wrong, and the fucker's gonna burn in hell for it."

It was the first time they had spoken about the Kongessa mission in years. After all the official proceedings, both men, the only survivors of the tragedy, had wordlessly agreed never to mention it again. It was done. Gone. In the past.

But the memory of that blood-soaked jungle haunted O'Rourke every day. Doubt about the decisions made and the actions taken gnawed at his mind. He had seen a lot of terrible things, *done* a lot of terrible things. But what had happened in the tiny African nation had shaken him to the core, changed the very essence of who he was.

It had changed Gibbs too.

"You're nothing like him," his boss said. "What happened in Boston isn't the same. Not even close."

"I made a call. A decision."

"Yeah, you made the right one."

"I shot a child! In the head! Twice!" O'Rourke was on his feet, scorching coffee soaking his jeans and a broken cup on the floor. Only he didn't remember moving. Didn't remember dropping his cup.

He closed his eyes and drew several long breaths deep into his lungs, just like that irritating psychiatrist had shown him.

"That *child* was seconds away from detonating a bomb," Gibbs reminded him. "Seconds away from killing hundreds of innocent people on that subway. You know what the tabloids called you? What the people they interviewed called the masked Special Forces soldier who saved their lives? A hero. A goddamn fucking hero."

"Well, I don't feel like a hero."

"Because you ain't one," Gibbs said. O'Rourke turned back to him, stung by his honesty. Gibbs shrugged. "You're just a man, doing his job and doing it damn well. Just because it was a hard choice, Rudy, don't make it the wrong choice."

O'Rourke brushed excess coffee from his jeans, the flesh beneath tender. "Tell that to that boy's parents." His words were soft, little more than a whisper, yet Gibbs caught them as though he'd shouted.

"That boy was a suicide bomber," he replied.

"That boy was a radicalised, brainwashed ten-year-old with a loving family that misses him. I took him away from them."

"It was too late for the little fucker," Gibbs spat. "The evil motherfuckers who groomed him killed him long before you got there. Hell, he was seconds away from blowing himself up as well!"

"I know!" O'Rourke snapped, punching the wooden leg of the swing chair. "I know all that, Laurie. But it doesn't make it any easier. Every time I close my eyes, I'm back in that subway tunnel, pulling the trigger. Only, it's not some random ten-year-old kid. It's Petey."

He wiped tears from his face, knowing Gibbs would be inwardly ridiculing his weakness. "And I just keep thinking, if that was Petey, if my boy had been brainwashed like that, I would hate the man who put him down. Who didn't even give him a chance.

"I saw that kid's eyes a second before my bullet blasted a hole between them. They were the same eyes I see every time Petey has a nightmare, every time Lyla wakes up confused, not knowing where she is. Great big innocent eyes filled with terror. But when I go to Petey's room or pluck Lyla out of her cot, I see something else. Love. Hope.

"That kid was terrified before he even knew I was there. Before he saw my gun. He was trapped in a nightmare . . . and instead of going to him, of giving him hope and love, I put him down."

He shook his head, the silence between them thick.

"You know, when I first joined the team," O'Rourke continued, "Landry told me something. He told me that every man has his limit. A line he will not cross. Not for his country, not even for the greater good."

"And that's what's got you thinking about Kongessa again?" Gibbs asked.

"I've never stopped thinking about Kongessa. About what happened there. But now, I think I get it. He found his line, and, orders be damned, he would not cross it."

"Our job is to follow orders. To do things others can't, to protect this country."

"But my orders led me to cross that line . . . I can't go any further down that path."

Gibbs' gaze shifted to him, those dark orbs dragging him into a black hole from which O'Rourke felt sure no light emanated. "I need you to go down that path one more time, Rudy. For old time's sake."

O'Rourke laughed, but the sound was devoid of humour. "I knew you weren't here just to check up on me." He shook his head. "It's been three months since Boston, and you've never once checked in."

"You got tagged on the shoulder," Gibbs argued. "I knew you weren't about to drop dead anytime soon. Besides, you needed space. Time. I gave you that. But now I-"

"Need me," O'Rourke cut in. Then he shook his head, pacing down the centre of the lawn. When he reached the fence, he turned back. "No. I'm out."

"You've been my Second for years. We've been through some shit together."

"And so has most of the team," O'Rourke argued.

"Not like us. You and me, we're the last of the old guard."

"And now it's time to make way for new blood," O'Rourke countered. "Lake would make a hell of a Second. Or Sykes."

"I don't need Lake or Sykes. I need you."

O'Rourke refused to meet the other man's gaze, his own eyes drifting to the house, to the silhouettes of his wife and kids behind the frosted glass of the bathroom window.

"I'm sorry, Boss," he said.

Gibbs followed his gaze, and O'Rourke knew what was coming, the same argument they'd had several times.

"I told you having a family would make you weak."

"I'm not getting into this," O'Rourke replied, shaking his head.

"You're a warrior, Rudy," Gibbs snarled. "You belong on the battlefield, not changing diapers."

"You know what I am? I'm a dad! Those three people up there, they don't make me weak. They're not a vulnerability. They're my strength. They've given me a reason to keep fighting all these years."

"Then keep fighting now!"

"I can't-"

"It's a Code Black mission, Rudy!" Gibbs cut him off. The words worked like a blow to the stomach, snatching the air out of him. "That's why I need you. Lake and Sykes and the others, they're good. But I don't need good; I need *you*. I need someone who knows my mind better than I do, who knows what action I'll take before I take it."

"A Code Black?" O'Rourke repeated, his voice little more than a whisper. His team was called in to secure US interests around the world. Their missions were so clandestine that nobody bothered with codes and threat levels – all their missions involved the highest threat level.

Except for a Code Black.

The highest classification was a warning of a clear and imminent attack on US soil with the likelihood of mass casualties, usually but not exclusively reserved for nuclear, chemical or biological threats. It also gave his team carte blanche to do whatever it took to neutralise the threat.

"I've not got all the details yet," Gibbs explained. O'Rourke knew he was breaking protocol and the law by revealing information to someone who had declined to join the mission. "A group of scientists have developed some sort of 'doomsday' weapon – we need to secure it before it is used against us."

"And I guess there are other interested parties?" O'Rourke asked.

Gibbs nodded slowly. "There's chatter," he admitted. "The powers-that-be reckon the weapon could be used in an imminent attack on American soil."

O'Rourke couldn't stop his eyes drifting once more towards his house. Zoey and the kids were back downstairs now, his wife's lithe shape flitting behind the sunlit reflection on the kitchen window.

Gibbs noticed. "You reckon they're your strength?" he asked. "Then lean on that strength now. If this weapon is used, who knows the target? Could be right here in New Orleans. Right in your backyard. If your family's your reason to fight, then fight!"

Heart racing, O'Rourke felt the urge to rush into the house, tell Zoey to get the kids on the next flight to her sister's in Madrid, grab his always-packed kitbag and race off with Gibbs and the team.

Instead, he took a deep breath and then let it out slowly. "You know what?" he asked, refusing to take his eyes away from his family. "Since Boston, I've realised they're more than just a reason to fight . . . they're a reason to live. They're a reason to live *with* myself. And I can barely do that right now. My hands are covered in blood, and if this mission is so big and important, I'll be washing them in even more blood by the end. How many more innocent lives will I be expected to take for the greater good, huh?"

Gibbs studied him with all the emotion of a coiled viper – his face remained unchanged, but the menace exuded from every pour.

"The target's in the jungle," he said. "There'll be no collateral. The only blood you'll be getting under your pretty, manicured fingernails will be of the guilty motherfuckers threatening our country." He paused, then held out his hand to him. "What do you say, Rudy? Let's save the world together, one last time?"

O'Rourke reached for the other man's hand-

"Daddy? Can we play ball now?"

Petey's voice was followed by the whistle of a baseball searing through the air like a bullet. Without removing his eyes from Gibbs' face, O'Rourke removed his hand from the other man's and snatched the ball from mid-air.

"I'm sorry," he said to Gibbs, daring him to argue. Then he turned to his son and lobbed the ball back at him. "Sure thing, Sport," he called.

Without a word, Gibbs slipped by him and down the garden path. O'Rourke focussed all his attention on Petey as he raced towards him, grappling him into a bear hug. But, as Gibbs closed the garden gate behind him, he called out.

"Wheels up at twelve hundred. Belle Chasse." Then he was gone.

Petey held his baseball bat out to his father. "You wanna bat?"

17:

JAMAICA, 1727

"**MISS** Emily!"

The voice was distant. Like an echo carried across a storm-tossed sea, lost to the howl of wind and waves.

"Miss Emily!"

She tried to swim towards the voice, to reach for it, but the storm's roar was too great.

"You must wake up!"

Wake up?

Only then did Emily Hamilton realise she was asleep. With a final surge of mental wherewithal, she crashed through the black storm in her mind and stumbled into a living hell.

She lay at the bottom of a deep shaft. An old well, she presumed. It must have been boarded up and covered by earth long ago, an accidental trap waiting for an unsuspecting victim. She felt oddly grateful for the lances of pain shooting up her left leg, informing her that her body, trapped beneath the rotten timber and heaps of soil, was still attached to her head.

That was small comfort, however, as consciousness reasserted itself more fully. Through the haze of her vision and the thick plumes of dust, she just made out the small shape of Charles Banks. He hung over the edge of the newly formed hole, his face a mask of terror.

That was when Emily realised the storm's roar had not faded on waking. In fact, it grew louder, a howl of rage, a hunger that could not be abated, a wall of flame silhouetting Banks' desperate frame. The naval officer glanced back.

"Where in God's name is that rope?" he bellowed.

Beyond him, Emily could see shapes rushing to and fro, a mad scramble of activity accompanied by grunts, groans and the angry hiss of water flash boiling to steam.

Oh, good heavens, she thought, fighting a tide of panic. She realised that the fire that Banks' people had been directing across the sugar cane field had quickly advanced on the hidden well. Despite the plantation workers' best efforts, it was evident that they had failed to douse the flames or redirect the fire away from her position.

"Miss Emily, reach for me," Banks shouted down to her, stretching out his arms.

No rope then, she realised.

"You must reach for me. Now!"

Fear drove a surge of strength through Emily. She cried out as she pushed against the debris entombing her. It didn't shift at first, but a second effort freed her enough to slide out and stagger to her feet. White-hot needles seemed to pierce her ankle and snake up her leg, but she fought through the pain and reached for Banks' hand. She fell about five handspans short and stumbled back against the jagged walls.

"Again!" Banks snapped, wriggling his upper body further into the opening. But a glance behind him etched a picture of terror upon his face. "Hurry!"

This time Emily jumped, arms stretched out as much as possible. Banks leaned as far over as he dared. Their hands met, clasped around each other, and Emily felt relief rush through her.

Banks pulled while Emily struggled for a foothold on the wall. But every time she found one, the rocks and earth gave way, tumbling back into the hole.

"Come on!" Banks snapped, panic shifting into anger. He turned to look behind him- and let out a gasp far less masculine sounding than Emily supposed he had intended.

Beyond her would-be-saviour, Emily saw the wall of fire, only yards away. Sweat poured from Banks' forehead, splashing down on her. His palm grew slick, difficult to grip.

"Sweet Lord," Banks cried, then he glared back down at her. "Let go."

Whatever sense of relief Emily had felt moments ago evaporated as surely as the hiss of water the plantation workers still used to try and control the flames.

"What?" she gasped. "No. Pull me up." She struggled to climb higher, only then realising she had lost her shoes. The rocky wall savaged her feet, ripping skin and drawing blood. But still, they conspired to deny her an escape route.

As did Charles Banks.

"Let go," he growled. Survival instinct tore through any illusions of heroism. He tried to shake Emily free and succeeded in dislodging one hand. She held firm with the other, clawing at the wall once more in an effort to climb.

"Let go!" Banks shouted, his voice high pitched, his eyes wide. He struggled to pull himself up but lacked the core strength to haul Emily with him. The fire licked at the soles of his leather boots.

"Let go!" he screamed, smashing Emily's remaining hand against the sharp stones of the hole's wall. She shrieked as bones snapped and blood gushed, reflexively releasing her grip.

Banks was gone before she even hit the ground, trying to bend her knees and absorb the impact. Her injured ankle gave way, and she crumpled into a heap. A sob escaped her throat.

No, she told herself. *You're stronger than this!*

She staggered back to her feet and fell against the wall, digging her fingers and toes in. She climbed about a foot high and then fell, swearing at her weakened ankle. She tried again, but the stony soil betrayed her, sending her back into the pit once more.

"Fuck!" she screamed in frustration, a strange flash of her father admonishing her for such unladylike language.

"Fuck you!" she shot at her father's phantom. "And fuck you!" she screamed up the hole at the coward who had abandoned her.

The wall of flame now circled two-thirds of the shaft's entrance. Searing heat spat down, and hissing embers scarred her flesh. Then, like a curtain drawing across the window of salvation, the wall of fire met on the far side, completely encircling her.

Emily fell back, shielding her face and head. The shaft's walls, even the ground beneath her feet, exuded heat, turning the pit into an oven.

She wouldn't just burn to death, she realised, fighting back a wave of nausea. *I'm going to literally be roasted.*

The air grew thin, nothing but a dry, hot sensation as she gulped it in. The heat drained her in seconds, sucking all energy from her body. Even the tears she cried vanished instantly, her eyes as dry as any desert.

Then, falling back upon the pile of debris, her lifeforce spent, she glanced up at the oddly beautiful curtain of red, yellow and orange fire. A dark shape formed within its heart, a black silhouette. And, with a final, frustrated sob, she realised that Death had come to claim her.

18:

THE LABYRINTH, SARISARIÑAMA TEPUI, VENEZUELA

"**CAN** we get out of here yet?"

Alverez shot Juan a look of irritation. "Stop being such a pussy, Emilio. They're already dead-they're not going to hurt you."

Emilio Juan glanced at the thousands of dead faces glaring back at him while clutching the gold crucifix dangling around his neck.

"Come on," Alverez said, glancing up from his tablet. Its screen cast an otherworldly glow across the Venezuelan's face, stressing its hard contours. "I want to check out that shaft before reporting the all-clear."

Juan groaned. "The structural integrity of this tunnel is okay," he argued. "We've installed the rescue gantry and winch . . . can't we just get out of here?"

Alverez rolled his eyes. "Do I have to pull rank?"

Juan sighed. While his friend jested, he was a *Maestro Técnico de Segunda,* or Second Technical Master, of the National Bolivarian Militia of Venezuela. He did, therefore, outrank Juan, a Third Technical Master.

The pair had been assigned to Sargento Raphael del Vega's contingent of militiamen on Sarisariñama because of their architectural speciality rather than any fighting skill, much to their boss's irritation. It had fallen to them to check the condition of the Labyrinth's tunnels, ensuring the safety of the archaeological team. Del Vega had ordered them into the skull-lined corridor for just that purpose.

Using a drone, they had conducted a visual survey of the tunnel from the far side of the crumbled partition wall. Then they had dropped the small flying machine through the hole in the floor that one of the archaeologists had fallen through earlier.

The water-filled chamber was silent.

Confident that two of the ceiling's rib-like arches had contained the collapse of the tunnel floor, Juan and Alverez had erected the tripod and gantry.

The contraption looked like a giant metal

spider straddling the hole, a winch feeding a galvanised cable through a series of pulleys to dangle into the void. Cave rescuers and miners used similar devices to move personnel and equipment between levels. Here, an excavation team planned to use it later that day to retrieve whatever they found so fascinating below.

"Okay," Juan said. "Let's get it done with."

Alverez smiled, slapping his friend on the shoulder with one hand while using the other to tap the drone's controls on his tablet, powering up its four mini propellers. They followed it around the hole in the floor and deeper into the tunnel, Juan whipping his helmet-mounted touch across his surroundings.

Reaching the large door at the end of the tunnel, Alverez sent the drone shooting up the vertical shaft that opened above their heads. Juan shifted his gaze to the tablet screen, watching the visual feed from the quadcopter's camera as it flew up.

"Don't get tangled in the roots," he warned Alverez, receiving a growl in response. The dangling roots grew thicker the higher the drone went, water beads running down them. Glancing up, all Juan saw was a tiny dot of light thirty metres above.

"That's it," Alverez announced. "That's the top."

"What's that?" Juan asked, looking over the other man's shoulder and pointing at a dark void on the screen.

"Looks like another tunnel branching off the shaft," Alverez replied. "Let's see what's down there."

"Shouldn't we wait until one of the archaeologists are with us? The Scottish bitch will kill us if we damage anything."

But it was too late. The drone was already hurtling down the horizontal tunnel. Its torch highlighted walls that appeared natural rather than the artificial jigsaw pattern they had become accustomed to. Within seconds, however, the walls vanished, replaced by darkness.

Alverez brought the drone to a hover. Dust motes drifted through its torch beam.

"What's going on?"

"I think it's in another chamber," Alverez replied, panning the drone around. "It must be massive because I can't see its walls or ceiling."

"Shit," Juan cursed, staring at the screen. "Where's the tunnel we flew through?"

"I don't know; I can't see anything." Alverez flew the drone back in the direction it had come, its beam hitting something and spilling across the obstacle.

"Del Vega will kill us if we lose it."

"I know," Alverez snapped.

"Whoa! What was that?" Juan asked, his heart

rate elevating again.

"What?"

"Something just flew across the beam."

"It's just a bat."

Juan remembered that the archaeological team had reported disturbing a colony of bats.

Before he could comment further, another flying creature shot through the beam, followed by another and another. The object that the beam had fallen upon began to move. It writhed and twisted before exploding outwards, unleashing a terrifying, high-pitched scream that echoed through the tunnels and turned Juan's blood cold.

"Shit!" Alverez panicked as darkness swept over the drone, knocking it and spinning it around in a circle, out of control. Its spiralling light corkscrewed through the gloom to illuminate flashes of movement. Bats were everywhere, flitting in and out of view, tens of thousands of them swirling around and around.

"Get down!" Juan cried, yanking Alverez to the ground as the noise from the shaft grew louder, and a deluge of impenetrable darkness swept down to consume them.

19:

UNESCO BASE CAMP, SARISARIÑAMA TEPUI, VENEZUELA

"**MY** working theory is that the Black Death followed a Moon Mask myth here," King said. Despite an audience several dozen strong, his attention was fixed solely on Juliet McKinney. She stood within the centre of her camp like a Roman orator addressing the Senate.

Or a dictator usurping control of it, he thought.

"And here he found a piece of it," McKinney finished for him. The sweat running down King's face wasn't entirely down to the intense humidity. Even as he tried to ignore them, he felt the eyes of his friends and colleagues boring into him.

"But," the Scot continued, "he got trapped in that chamber and died? Rather a pathetic end to the legacy of the Black Death, wouldn't you say?"

"Okay, say we believe all that," Yousef spoke up. "What does it have to do with your Progenitor Theory? I thought that was all about ancient human origins or something?"

"It is," King agreed, nodding. "The Moon Mask myth is not unique to the Bouda, nor even the African continent," he explained. "We find versions of it in cultures, both ancient and modern, across the globe, passed down through folk tales and oral traditions or recorded in cave art and even in textiles."

"Interpreted according to the Universal Motif Language," McKinney added, mockery in her tone. "A 'translation process' you and your father developed specifically to warp versions of history to fit your larger thesis."

"The academic community accepts the UML as a valid tool for interpreting abstract human thought," Nadia said, speaking for the first time. She hung behind King and Sid, keeping to the shade of the larger tents at her back. "No such tool is perfect. Any conclusion drawn from it is open to interpretation. Yet, other scholars have successfully applied its methodology outside the Kings' research."

Not even McKinney dared argue with the Russian's logic, so King continued. Sid shot her friend a quick smile, knowing how her statement bolstered her boyfriend's standing without endorsing his theory.

"One can find tales of fortune-telling masks throughout the Americas. Many of them are linked to stories about the moon," King said, stepping closer to his audience, impassioned by his own words. "Cultures in Australasia and the Pacific islands likewise have similar myths, as do many traditional societies in East and South East Asia. Even the Ancient Egyptian Book of the Dead talks about a powerful mask during *Zep Tepi*, The First Time. It drew its magic from the moon and may have given birth to a millennia-spanning tradition of death masks."

"And we can find all these fairy tales on your blog, no?" McKinney added, not bothering to hide her derision.

King ignored her. "My father and I have spent years unravelling these stories, many of which are admittedly obscure. But, while the specifics of each differ, the underlying theme is too niche a topic, too specific to have developed in so many cultures, in so many forms, coincidentally. A magical mask, often associated with the moon, which grants its wearer the gift of foresight."

"And so, the obvious answer is that this myth spread around the globe, transmitted by some prehistoric 'mother race'," McKinney concluded from memory. "Assisted by aliens and survivors of Atlantis, if one believes many of your Twitter followers."

"No," King snapped. He knew how his theory attracted pseudo-scientists. His father had called them 'pyram-idiots', a constant irritant, undermining the academic foundations upon which their work balanced. Such outlandish links to extra-terrestrials and godmen had led to recognised scientists rejecting what had once been an avid pursuit for a mother race. Ridicule awaited any who dared continue such research.

"No," King said again, calming himself. "An ancient people we term the 'Progenitors' are, my father and I proposed, a mother *culture*, not a mother race. They are a feasible, even *probable*, human society. Archaeological, anatomical and genetic evidence points to an African origin for modern humans. The first evidence for so-called 'modern human behaviour' also appears in Africa. Our Progenitor Theory, correctly called the *African Cultural Progenitor Diffusion Model*, or *Out of Africa 3*, takes this African origin focus to the next level. It suggests that one early group of people perfected several aspects of modern human behaviour before spreading it out of Africa."

King's speech was rolling now, an avalanche of information spilling out, regardless of his audience's attention level.

"These behaviours manifested themselves in several traits," he continued, "which we usually associate only with 'civilisations'. Social hierarchy, for instance. Monumental building techniques, sophisticated agricultural knowledge, and a written form of communication.

"The society was what we would consider a small city-state. The fundamental building blocks of civilisation were transmitted from this city during a series of migratory waves and cultural diffusion. Egypt and Mesopotamia first, then on to the rest of Asia, and eventually to Europe and the Americas."

"Despite insurmountable evidence suggesting such 'traits' developed independently in these areas?" McKinney laughed.

"Developed? Yes," King allowed. "Originated? No. Such developments came about because of 'cultural memory,' if you will, stored at a genetic level, an *instinctual* level in the brains of all human beings. Such cultural or genetic memory is a fundamental part of the human condition; it makes us human and sets us apart from other animals. That is why we see similar architectural forms, like pyramids, worldwide. It is why mythological motifs are replicated around the globe. Why a correlation can be drawn between, for instance, the Greeks' Cyclops, the oral traditions of the Saami of Scandinavia and the Apaches of North America."

McKinney huffed, as did several others, while a few looked on with cautious interest.

"These memories are often 'unlocked' by shamans and other individuals with a link to what they perceive as a spirit world during Altered States of Consciousness," King pushed on. "The genetic memory of the culture of the Progenitors is everywhere we look. That is why we find similar imagery in rock art in prehistoric Europe, Africa and Australasia. My father and I spent years compiling this evidence into a thorough, unified theory. We've gathered genetic, anatomic, historical, epigraphic, mythological and archaeological evidence. But what we needed to cement our theory was proof of the *physical* movement of these people."

"And the Moon Mask is that proof?" McKinney concluded.

"Yes," King said, eyes wide with enthusiasm. "That is why the Moon Mask, specifically the Bouda Moon Mask, has been so central to my career, to my entire life. Because, out of all the versions of the Moon Mask legends found from Africa to South America, it is the only one with a physical manifestation we can pursue archaeologically. A search for the man represented on that graffiti at Wassu, the last Great King of the Bouda. And that man lies buried beneath our feet, protected by crocodiles and God knows what else."

"How can you be so sure the skeleton you found is him?" Yousef asked.

Now it was King's turn to look in disbelief, as though the answer should be as apparent to his audience as it was to him. "A skeleton," he said slowly, as if to a child, "found alongside a matching 'gold' sword and dagger and wearing a mask?" The sea of faces staring back at him seemed less convinced. "Kha'um, the Black Death and the skeleton are the same person," he pressed. "That he found a piece of the Moon Mask, an originally African object, in a secret labyrinth in South America, offers credibility to the Bouda legend. Someone in deepest, darkest antiquity cast the original mask asunder and scattered it across the earth."

King opened his arms, imploring his colleagues to cast aside their conditioning by mainstream academia and open their minds to alternatives.

"This migratory process took hundreds or even thousands of years. But, as these 'progenitor' people spread from their city in Africa, along with a package of behavioural traits transmitted to the other developing cultures they encountered, they carried pieces of the mask and legends about it. These legends changed and shifted and distorted through time and cultural appropriation, but ultimately hark back to that original, core story." He glared at his colleagues, unable to understand why they didn't see what he saw.

"Ben," Sid whispered, squeezing his hand, but he pulled free and stepped towards the crowd.

"Don't you see what I'm saying?" he asked. "The Moon Mask's presence here proves the Progenitors existed. It rewrites the history of human civilisation."

Several people burst out in laughter, shaking their heads and shuffling away. Others at least had the decency to mask their smirks while two or three mulled his words over.

It surprised King that McKinney fell into the latter group.

But he sensed a trap.

"I agree," McKinney replied. "An ancient African object in an ancient South American ruin suggests contact between the two. But," she added, dropping the metaphorical axe. "So far, your evidence is entirely circumstantial. It is based solely on your unfiltered observations and interpretation of what's in that chamber. Masks litter Central and South America. From what I saw of the one you found, little about it seems traditionally African."

"The Moon Mask is a composite-"

"Furthermore, neither gold nor brass makes an effective weapon; they are too soft to use in combat and reserved for ritual."

"But-"

"Even though the indigenous people of South America did not possess metal weapons at the time of the Spanish Conquest," McKinney bulldozed over him. "They did possess the most sophisticated metallurgical industry of the ancient world. That they fashioned a sword and dagger out of gold or brass is nothing startling. And, as for your assumption that the individual is not local based on fragments of cloth and a supposed 'tricorn,' that remains one man's interpretation."

King's face screwed into a snarl, his scar blazing pinkish-red against his midnight skin.

"So, what are our options, *Doctor* King?" the professor pressed. "On the one hand, we have your theory. That our bony friend down there is an African king-slave-pirate who scoured the world searching for a magical time-travelling mask that was a gift from his gods and proves all the world's civilisations stem from a single source. Or, we have my theory: that he was most likely a human sacrifice, accorded the ritual apparatus – a ceremonial mask and weaponry – that his exalted position required. And," she added, face reddening as she allowed her ire back to the surface, "even if my theory is wrong, there are still a hundred and one better, far more plausible explanations for the presence of an *indigenous* person's remains, with *indigenous* material culture, in an *indigenous* ceremonial centre."

"Bats!"

The scream echoed across the mountaintop, cutting off King's response. He spun towards the source, his eyes widening at the sight of thousands of bats sweeping up and out of the black maw of Sima Humboldt and descending on the base camp.

20:

JAMAICA, 1727

THE figure of death materialised from the glaring fire.

Emily was too drained to scream as the wraith glided down towards her, growing ever larger, obscuring her vision.

The searing heat overwhelmed her senses. She didn't even feel the pain of roasting to death, nor the terror of the approaching figure reaching out for her.

Can this devil even take me to a worse hell than this? she wondered.

That devil came into view, and it was indeed Death. Only not the Death she had expected.

Looming above her was a giant of a man, arms as thick as branches, legs as strong as tree trunks. He had planted his feet on one side of the shaft, his hands on the other. He walked down the vertical hole like an enormous spider traversing a pipe.

The Black Death, Emily realised, recognising the enslaved man from earlier. Now, as then, his eyes locked onto hers. A thrill raced through her body, carried aloft on a wave of hope.

He ignored the heat, which must surely have been blistering the skin on his bare back. Then he released one hand from his pressure-perch and, without a word, grasped the front of Emily's dress. He heaved her up, a deep grunt the only indication of effort.

The Black Death's footing slipped, and Emily gasped. But, somehow, the giant held firm and pulled her to him. Instinctively, Emily reached out, wrapping her arms around his neck.

"Wrap your legs around me," the Black Death commanded. Emily obeyed, swinging her athletic body up and wrapping herself around him. She felt the hard contours of his muscular chest as he shifted his hand back onto the wall. With their faces only inches apart, and their sweat-soaked bodies tangled around one another, it was the most intimate embrace of her life.

Their eyes locked. His harboured the same intensity Emily had noted earlier, now also set with fierce determination. She realised that this man, this stranger, would not abandon her as Banks had.

Or like my father abandoning me to a life of misery just to pay off his debts. The thought came unbidden to her mind.

"Hold on," the Black Death told her. His voice reverberated like a thunder roll through his chest. Then, limbs spread-eagled across the well, Emily dangling from him, he made his ascent.

Flames raged above them, viper-like tongues lashing down, swirling with deadly desire. The Black Death's body shielded her, his resolve breathing new life through her exhaustion. She felt the skin on his back grow hotter and imagined it blistering under the intensity of the fire. Yet he showed no sign of panic. Every move of a limb, one above the other, was considered, planned, intended. One hand, then a foot; the next hand, another foot.

Progress seemed slow, as though Emily was trapped in molasses. Her arms and legs ached from holding onto her rescuer; each breath of thin, scalding air was more painful than the last. But they finally neared the top.

Then what? Emily wondered. A flaming prison completely encircled the hole. Yet she sensed the

Black Death had a plan.

Sure enough, just below the hole's rim, the Black Death mumbled something between clenched teeth that sounded like 'hold tight.' Then he released the pressure on his legs and swung upright, kicking out to stop him from crushing Emily against the wall. She yelped at the impact but held firm.

"Climb onto my back," the Black Death rumbled, his deep voice challenging to hear beneath the roaring flames.

"What? But your back is burnt-"

"Do it," he snapped, grunting at the effort of gripping the wall, supporting her weight and fighting the pain of his seared flesh. Indeed, as Emily obeyed and scrambled around his torso, cursing her ridiculous dress, the acrid scent of burnt flesh assaulted her nostrils. His skin was slick, though she didn't know whether it was just sweat or a mixture of sweat and blood.

"Whatever happens next, do not let go," the Black Death told her. Then he moved so fast that Emily's exhausted mind struggled to keep up. With surprisingly catlike agility considering his enormity, the man lashed out. He snagged a bucket Emily saw dangling from a metal chain below the rim. Water sloshed within, and she realised that her rescuer must have stashed it there before making his descent.

In one fluid motion, swinging with surprising ease, he used his momentum to haul himself out of the hole and into the fire.

Emily screamed as the flames roared around her, catching the frills of her dress and singing her golden hair. But the Black Death had hurled the bucket of water in front of them. It flash boiled on impact with the fire, but it opened a corridor between the flames for a split second. The Black Death barrelled down that tunnel, not uttering a sound even as the fire danced across his naked flesh.

Then, in a blinding flash, they were free of the flames. The Black Death reached around and plucked Emily from his back, throwing her to the ground.

She was too stunned to react as Banks, Jessica, Francesca and a small army of workers bundled around her, dragging her further from the flames. She was lost in a tangle of black and white limbs, hands groping her, patting fire from her clothes, dousing her in water, and asking dozens of questions.

But her gaze broke through the mass of bodies and locked onto a single figure standing alone before the wall of flame. Then, with dreadful slowness, the Black Death dropped to his knees. He sought her gaze through the chaos before him. A thin smile parted his lips just as he toppled face-first to the ground.

21

UNESCO BASE CAMP, SARISARIÑAMA TEPUI, VENEZUELA

"**YOU** have got to be kidding me," Nathan Raine groaned as he watched thousands of bats spewing from Sarisariñama's largest sinkhole. The spectacle was almost identical to his nightmare, vision, Soul Flight, or whatever the hell Maria had subjected him to. Each bat was lost amidst the manic flutter of the mass.

Just as the inky, tar-like darkness of his nightmare had undulated and twisted across the summit of the table mountain, so too did this swarm of flying creatures.

Raine had been preparing to land when the bats had burst from Sima Humboldt's depths. Instead, he'd thrown the Huey into a hover and watched the spectacle.

An endless ocean of green, broken only by the snaking meanders of the Orinoco's tributaries, spread from the base of Sarisariñama's cliffs. Raine struggled to push the image of that rich green carpet, rotting to darkness, from his mind.

"You must not go to the Dark Mountain," Maria's warning echoed through his memory.

Raine shook his head, pushing through the after-effects of whatever concoction the Ye'kuana woman had fed him to analyse the situation with trained detachment.

The UNESCO expedition basecamp was a sprawling canvas city, nestled with Roman precision into a natural clearing between the sinkhole and the north-eastern clifftop. Nine large, marquee-like structures formed the perimeter of the camp. Five were science labs, while one housed communication equipment and computer servers. Another contained piles of general excavation equipment; one acted as the de-facto 'headquarters,' reserved for McKinney and her inner circle. The fifth was the social hub, a large mess tent where the team spent most of their off-duty time.

Lined up in neat rows between them were dozens of khaki-green, two-person tents and a handful of floodlights. Rows of solar panels and large batteries, providing the expedition's power demands, lined a path leading from the Mess Tent towards what passed as the helipad in a neighbouring clearing.

It looked like humanity had invaded one of the world's last unconquered natural strongholds. But the expedition planners had designed the enterprise to have almost zero lasting impact on the environment. Everything would be removed once the mission was over. Only one piece of equipment was not powered by solar energy: the mechanical winch lift that raised and lowered a metal cage down the sinkhole to the Labyrinth's doorway.

That same doorway now disgorged an endless cloud of winged animals. Like a gyrating shoal of fish, they sped up the sinkhole's steep sides and flooded through the camp, crashing into tents and knocking over equipment. People fled the frenzied creatures, screaming as they raced down the avenues between tents, seeking shelter under canvas, waiting for the deluge to end.

But, as Raine watched, no such end was in sight. Whatever roost had been disturbed must have been massive; he had witnessed large swarms of bats on his previous stopovers but nothing like what he saw now. Millions of them must have travelled through the tunnel system before bursting into daylight. But instead of dispersing across the rainforest, they swirled over the basecamp, terrorising it. There was nothing anyone could do about it.

"If there's one thing I hate more than clichés," Raine said to himself, pulling his bathrobe tighter, "it's coincidences . . . and so far this morning, there's been too many of both."

Instead of waiting to see if his vision came true, Raine plunged the helicopter into a steep dive, sweeping towards the summit.

22:

UNESCO BASE CAMP, SARISARIÑAMA TEPUI, VENEZUELA

THE collective pounding of millions of wings in the air was deafening as King, Sid, and Nadia encountered their second swarm of bats that morning.

They were everywhere, blotting out the sun, turning day to night, filling their vision, overloading their senses. Individual specimens were difficult to make out amidst the writhing whole.

"This is impossible," Sid said. They took shelter just inside Lab 5's opening, where most of those gathered to witness King's showdown with McKinney had scrambled. They had zipped the door shut, but the plastic windows offered a dazzling view of the swarm pounding against the sturdy canvas structure.

One specimen splatted against the window in front of the trio, making them yelp and jump back. Bared teeth gnashed at them as the bat hammered against the plastic before being swept up into the roiling mass once more, allowing its companions to dive-bomb the cowering scientists.

"Everybody, stay calm!" McKinney shouted to the tent's occupants. King spun to see the redhead over-acting in front of a smartphone's camera and rolled his eyes.

"The largest colony of bats ever recorded in Austin, Texas," she told her improvised cameraman, "was estimated to be over forty million strong, and I can well believe a similar number has descended upon us now-"

Thunder drowned out her words, and the Lab tent shook.

"It's Raine!" someone shouted from the far side of the tent. King's eyes rolled further still before focussing through the swarm at the American's helicopter. He swung it like a pendulum, slicing through the mass of flitting darkness. For an instant, bats scattered, and a slither of blue sky appeared overhead before the curtain drew in once more.

Raine swept skywards before swinging the Huey around on itself and driving down into the churning miasma again. This time, King watched as the mass of bats, as if possessed of a single mind, parted before the helicopter's passage, like an icebreaker slicing through frozen mush.

"What's he doing?" Sid asked.

Nadia raised an eyebrow. "Scientists recently deployed an aerial drone to fly amongst a swarm of eight hundred thousand bats in New Mexico," she disgorged her encyclopaedic knowledge. "Not a single bat impacted the machine. In fact, they purposely flew around it, leading the scientists to suggest that their echolocation abilities permitted them to detect and avoid foreign objects in flight." She turned her attention to the would-be-cameraman who had shifted his attention to her. "I prefer not to be filmed."

"We'll edit that out," McKinney bulldozed over her demand, jumping back into the shot. "Our helicopter pilot must know that," she continued, "and is using his skills to scatter the swarm away from us."

"Or he's just being an over-confident knob charging into a situation with no clue what he's doing," King added.

McKinney glowered at him. "We'll edit that out too."

"They're in a Lab tent!" Yousef shouted as the

helicopter made another pass, clearing the view of the mountain top to reveal hundreds of the creatures thrashing around inside one of the Labs, its door left unzipped. Even from his awkward viewing angle, King could see equipment crashing to the ground amid sparks of electricity.

"The mask," he gasped, terror clutching his heart tighter than during his encounter with the crocodiles. He recognised which lab was under attack: Lab 2, where he had left the Moon Mask for later study.

Without hesitation, King tore up the zip, the din of pounding wings and helicopter rotors washing inside, along with half a dozen winged denizens, eliciting cries of horror from Lab 5's occupants.

"Ben, wait!" Sid screamed, but King was already through the opening and charging into the maelstrom of darkness.

"WHAT the hell?" Raine cursed, noting the figure dash from the relative safety of one of the labs and charge into the chaos, recognising the individual as Benjamin King.

He refused to entertain the notion of Maria's prophecy, especially when he noticed a second human figure appear from a tent.

"Sid," he said. "What the hell are you doing?" While bats were not ordinarily aggressive, something had whipped these into a frenzy of claws and teeth.

Without hesitation, Raine pushed down on the collective while manipulating the cyclic, forcing the Huey to pitch forward and roll to the left, descending into the darkest mass at the swarm's core.

DARKNESS enveloped King, but he staggered on, blinded by flitting wings and pounded by large, furry bodies, desperate to reach the mask.

"Ben!" Sid's scream cut through the din of beating wings. He had heard her shout after him as he left Lab 5, but this noise was different, filled with panic.

He spun around, but all he could see was a wall of bats.

"Sid?" he shouted, only for a large specimen to slam into the side of his head, knocking him to the ground. He rolled onto his belly, flinging his arms around to deter further attacks, but it was no use.

The thudding propellers roared above the beating wings as Raine brought his helicopter down low to the ground, just above the roof of the tallest tent. The cloud of darkness retreated like a veil drawing back, and sunlight glared down.

King rolled to his side, shielding his eyes from flying debris, tossed up in the chopper's downdraft, and searched for Sid. She lay on the ground five metres away, curled into the foetal position, unfurling her limbs as she noticed the momentary reprieve from the bats' assault.

King ran to her, helping her to her feet.

"What the hell are you doing?" she demanded, face twisted with rage. Her midnight hair swirled around her, and dozens of tiny claws had slashed her skin.

"Come on," King ordered, ignoring her complaint and pulling her behind him. Raine kept the helicopter above them, tracking their movements, its downdraft operating as a protective bubble, sweeping the swarm out of their way.

Reaching the open doorway to Lab 2, King yanked Sid inside. Bats swirled around the enclosed space, knocking over equipment and tables. Their entrapment whipped them into a greater frenzy than those outside.

"Ben, it's not safe in here," Sid shouted. But King ignored her and the shift in the helicopter's tempo as it ascended away, shuddering the canvas structure on its passage.

"There it is," he gasped, pushing through thrashing bats. He had left the mask on a canvas-covered workbench, but it was now upended, the mask lying face-down on the groundsheet. He scrambled towards it and scooped it up, a wave of relief washing through his core and spreading through his limbs. For a split second, he forgot about their predicament.

"Great, but now we're trapped!"

Sid's observation was correct. The black curtain had fallen outside the Lab's entrance once more, and they both knew they stood no chance of making it back to one of the other sealed labs.

King scanned the tent, searching for anything that could help. "Quickly," he said, dragging Sid to the upturned workbench, unzipping its canvas wraparound and yanking out its shelves. "Get in," he told Sid, pushing her inside before scrambling into the confined space with her, wrenching the zip closed.

Beyond their canvas cocoon, the bats continued their relentless assault with no sign of letting up. Rather, like a remorseless hoard of barbarians descending upon a war-torn city, they redoubled their efforts and retargeted all their aggression on the upturned workbench.

All King and Sid could do was close their eyes and scream.

23:

UNESCO BASE CAMP, SARISARIÑAMA TEPUI, VENEZUELA

AS soon as King and Sid were inside one of the labs, Raine pulled up and hurtled away from the base camp.

Ploughing headlong into the maelstrom with no idea what he was doing, he had been lucky enough to avoid colliding with any of the nocturnal creatures.

Now, however, he had a plan.

Gaining altitude, Raine thundered across the summit, making the five-hundred-metre hop from the camp to the sinkhole in seconds. *Sima Humboldt's* yawning expanse hung below him, its base and sides choked by vegetation. The ugly mechanical scar of the lift clung to the sinkhole's upper lip. A series of metal cables fed down the three-hundred-and-fifty-metre-tall cliffs to a narrow catwalk affixed outside the ancient doorway just over halfway down.

Bats belched from the doorway. They followed one another in an almost orderly fashion up the sinkhole's wall and across the summit. They looked more like a disciplined line of ants than the manic swarm they mutated into upon reaching the camp. It was as though the UNESCO scientists were the winged army's target, their final battlefield. Even several million strong, they showed no sign of letting up their assault.

"Here goes nothing," Raine said. "Or everything," he added, then he dropped the Huey towards the lip of the sinkhole, directly into the bats' flight route. He altered pitch, lifting the helicopter's nose skyward. The full brunt of its propellers' downdraft pounded down as the creatures ascended.

He knew the battered, Vietnam War-era chopper wouldn't stand up to much of an impact, especially if a bat hit its cobbled-together rotor assembly. Hovering over the green abyss of the sinkhole, there would be no opportunity to bail out.

With relief, he watched as what he hoped would happen manifested itself. Cutting their line of attack in half, the leading mammals of the second wave swept around, doubling back on themselves. Instead of following their kin to the base camp, they swirled and thrashed within the confines of *Sima Humboldt's* three-hundred-metre-wide chasm. Their numbers swelled as more continued to pour out of the

Labyrinth.

Raine kept guard of the sinkhole's perimeter, rolling left or right to deter any bats from escaping. Moments later, a tongue of flame lashed out from beneath the Huey, followed by sporadic bursts of machine gunfire.

Raine glanced down to note five of the Venezuelan militiamen below, led by the flame-thrower-wielding Raphael del Vega. They followed his example, taking up guard positions along the sinkhole's north-western rim.

"Good work, Raine," the sergeant's gruff voice echoed through his radio headset, tuned to the expedition's standard frequency.

"Why, thank you," Raine replied, mimicking the other man's patronisation. However, despite a mutual dislike of one another, they both forced professionalism into their tones. "Is anyone in the tunnels?"

"The excavation teams had broken for lunch," del Vega replied. *"I've been a little too busy to do a headcount, but everyone should have been topside except for two of my men. I can't get any response from them,"* he added with a growl, unleashing another line of fire and incinerating a swath of bats near the edge of the sinkhole.

Raine understood the sergeant's frustration at the thought of losing two of his team. While not aggressive, he feared the claws and teeth of so many bats would have shredded alive anyone caught in the confined tunnel system.

"I'm sure they'll be fine," Raine replied, receiving nothing but an incoherent grumble in response.

THE LABYRINTH, SARISARIÑAMA TEPUI, VENEZUELA

"**MOVE,** move, move!" Alverez screamed. Juan flailed about, thrashing his arms around his head. He'd already dropped to his hands and knees, crawling back up the sloping skull-lined corridor behind his fellow militiaman. But, despite hugging the ground, he still felt hundreds of the winged creatures slamming into him. Only his heavy-duty military fatigues and Kevlar armour protected him from their claws.

"We're nearly there!" Alverez shouted, his voice almost lost beneath the din.

Where? Juan wondered, knowing they were deep inside the tunnel system. They had nowhere to go to escape the seemingly endless barrage of flying mammals.

Then he got his answer.

"No," he snapped.

Alverez turned to look at him, his face cut and bloody. "You have a better idea?"

Juan glanced from his friend to the hole in the floor. The rescue winch's tripod still straddled it, a cable dangling into the darkness below.

"Didn't you hear what the scientists said? Crocodiles and . . . and something that ate a crocodile? I mean, what the fuck eats a crocodile?"

Alverez reached out and dragged him closer. "Emilio, listen to me," he said. "We can't stay here. We can't get out of the tunnels. This is our only chance. Del Vega said the crocs were lethargic until King disturbed them."

"So?"

A bat slammed into Alverez's face, knocking him backwards. He smacked it away, cursing, and dropped even lower to the ground.

"So we don't disturb them," he finished. "And if we do, we're at least better prepared than they were," he added, patting his MP5 submachine gun. "Okay?"

Juan struggled to get his breathing back under control. "Okay," he said. Then he watched as Alverez lowered himself into the hole, his head dropping from sight. Juan was just about to follow him when something caught his eye, a shape moving amidst the flurry of winged bodies.

A white face glared at him through the gloom and a strange sound carried above the pounding of wings.

Sari . . . Sari . . .

THE sight below Raine was both awesome and terrifying. The entire yawning chasm of the *Sima Humboldt* sinkhole was alive with a gyrating swirl of bats. They swung around and around, a churning vortex of darkness. And still it grew, larger and larger, like a storm-ravaged reservoir ready to explode through its dam.

"Del Vega, this isn't working," he called through his headset. "Have your men fall back, take cover."

"No," the militiaman shot back. *"We make a stand here – they'll breach the far side of the sinkhole and fly away-"*

Just as the Venezuelan predicted, the heaving morass of inky black did indeed breach the sinkhole's sides, their numbers swelling so much that it could no longer contain them. But rather than flying away, they plumed out like a volcano spewing forth. For a moment, it seemed like the entire army of flying mammals drew up into the sky like an immense wall, blotting out the sun. Then, like a tidal wave breaking against the shore, it fell upon them.

"Shit!" Raine cursed. He yanked the Huey's cyclic to port, trying to turn away from the sinkhole. The green expanse of the rainforest below Sarisariñama flitted into his vision as he aimed towards the mountain's cliff edge.

But then the first impact came, jolting through the helicopter's frame. A burst of red, splattered by the rotors' downdraft, spewed across his windshield, followed by another and another. Vibrations racked through the aircraft, and he realised that bats were flying into its propellers. While the blades minced the tiny creatures like a blender, their sheer numbers quickly overwhelmed him.

Warning lights danced across his control panel, an opera of alerts and manic beeps announcing a plethora of damage. Then something changed; something shifted. The vibrations, the noise, the sudden lack of power. Even the line of Sarisariñama's cliff edge shifted, sinking lower on the horizon.

Raine realised he was tipping backwards. The propellers slowed, the engines stalled, and the momentum dragged him towards the sinkhole, gravity pulling him deeper into the abyss.

"Shit!" he cried again as the battered Huey spun out of control, dropping into oblivion.

Just like Maria had shown him.

"No more moonshine for me," he vowed.

24:

UNESCO BASE CAMP, SARISARIÑAMA TEPUI, VENEZUELA

MOST other people would have panicked.

Nathan Raine was not most other people.

Even as his helicopter lost power and dropped into the yawning chasm of Sima Humboldt, the flash of the sinkhole's rim seeming to spin around the azure sky, his training kicked in.

Panic, he knew, was now his worst enemy.

The moment the Huey lost power, like all helicopters, the engine automatically disengaged from the main rotor, allowing it to spin freely. The upward flow of air through it kept it turning at an RPM that, under expert control, allowed it to glide into a landing using only residual kinetic energy. Like all helicopter pilots,

Raine had practised a powerless autorotative descent dozens of times.

But that's usually over open fields or well-equipped airbases, he thought. *Not confined sinkholes burrowing vertically into the heart of a mountain.*

He pushed self-doubt aside and instantly lowered the collective, reducing the Huey's drag and lift. Then he worked the antitorque pedals to adjust the tail rotor and pull out of an uncontrolled spin. As he plummeted, the blurred motion of the sinkhole walls slowed ever so slightly. But, with only three hundred metres from edge to edge, he had very little diagonal space to affect a safe autorotation landing on the sinkhole's floor. In an instant, he realised he would more likely crash into the far wall or slam into the ground at too great a speed.

"Fuck," he cursed, realising he had only one option: restart a stalled engine.

This isn't a Hollywood movie, Nate, he reminded himself. Regardless of what Pierce Brosnan-led Bond movies implied, most modern helicopters couldn't restart engines from their own starter motors in freefall. Indeed, the failsafe of a free-wheeling, automatically disengaging clutch disconnected the engine from the rotors.

His battered Huey, however, was anything but modern.

Here goes nothing.

Having regained some control, he manually re-engaged the chopper's old-fashioned, conventional clutch, effectively reconnecting the rotors to the engine. The blades' autorotation ground against the clutch, momentarily slowing their RPG. Without their kinetic energy supplying limited lift, the Huey dropped like a stone, the entire fuselage now spinning around within the sinkhole. But the increased descent then thrust more air up through the rotors, spinning them faster than before. Raine adjusted the aft cyclic and collective, bringing the nose up. Then he pumped twice on the gas and ignited the starter motor.

Seconds before impact with the rock-strewn vegetation at the sinkhole's base, the engines roared into life, driving the rotors at phenomenal speed and arresting his descent. Then he pulled up on the collective, adjusted the cyclic and worked the pedals, banking the Huey up and away from the sinkhole walls.

He burst out of the *Sima Humboldt* with an almost triumphant flourish, pitching hard and thundering away from the swirling vortex of bats that still rained havoc upon the base camp.

A cheer erupted inside the lab as the scientists sheltering there watched Raine's helicopter escape the sinkhole.

Even Nadia couldn't stop a smile of relief from curving her lips. It had only been seconds since she'd watched the tidal wave of bats hammer down onto the aircraft and it drop into the sinkhole. But it had felt like an eternity, the entire lab dropping to shocked silence. Even McKinney had the respect to shut up, presuming that Nathan Raine had perished in the accident.

Now, however, Raine's incredible escape reinvigorated them all. But, while most of the tent's occupants cheered and excitedly regurgitated the scene they'd just witnessed half a dozen times, Nadia remained silent at the door.

"It's not over yet," she whispered. Yousef, standing near her, caught her words. He turned to look out the plastic window with her. The second wave of bats seemed even bigger than the first, and it washed down over the camp like a flood. Nadia saw bursts of fire and heard the echo of automatic gunfire as del Vega and his men fought through the swarm.

"What do we do?" Yousef wondered.

"What *can* we do?" Jiao asked, joining their conversation. The young Chinese woman stared out at the maelstrom. "Is it me, or does it look like the bats are targeting Lab 2?"

"Maybe they're trying to get their mask back," Yousef joked.

Nadia had also noticed the strange concentration of the winged mammals swirling around the other science lab, a black, dense heart amidst the storm. She tried to hold back the worry she felt for King and Sid, knowing that standing here fretting would do them no good.

"We need to disperse the bats," she announced instead.

"Disperse them?" Yousef repeated. "How?"

"I have an idea."

"I have an idea," Nadia's voice crackled over Raine's headset. *"But I need to get to the equipment tent."*

"And, let me guess," Raine replied. "You need me to clear you a path?"

Hovering beyond the cliff edge, Raine looked back at the mountaintop. The base camp was almost totally lost beneath the black, undulating carpet now. But, while the stream of bats from within the sinkhole finally seemed to lessen to a trickle, the central mass showed no signs of shifting.

Raine checked his dashboard. While several warning lights still blinked, the Huey felt okay. It remained in a stable hover without any unexpected vibrations or noises suggesting more severe damage than he had hoped.

But he knew he'd been lucky. While the swarm had initially moved around the helicopter when he'd flown among them, that second wave had seemed more violent. Even now, they seemed more intent, more purposeful, focusing most of their attention on Lab 2, where King and Sid had fled.

During his flight from Carimara to Sarisariñama, McKinney had told him over the radio that King had found a mask. She wanted him to help recover more archaeological artefacts from a hidden chamber. And, try as he might, he couldn't shake the sense that this was all connected to the bats. And to Maria's prophecy.

Cajushawa *manifested himself in the form of a fanged face. With his army of odosha, his demons, he devoured the earth. The Face of* Cajushawa *remains on the mountain to this day, making the sound* sari . . . sari . . . *as he feasts upon the flesh of any who venture there.*

Raine opened his mouth, about to tell Nadia that it was too dangerous to fly amongst the bats again. There was no guarantee that they would part before him as they had before. Then he shut it again.

Maria really got in your head, he admonished himself.

Nathan Raine was many things, but he was no coward. He couldn't sit safely in his helicopter watching as the sheer weight of attacking bats crumpled the tents in which his friends sought shelter.

"Okay," he said. "Tell me what you need."

"ARE you ready?" del Vega asked.

Nadia adjusted her borrowed Kevlar vest and foul-smelling militia fatigues, then glanced at the Venezuelan. The sergeant stood a head taller than her, and she imagined she could fit two of her within the girth of his muscle-bound frame. Yet, despite how intimidating his size made him look, the floppy, cartoonish moustache covering his lips added a comedic element to his persona.

"Ready," Nadia acknowledged.

Del Vega and his team had only just made it to the relative safety of Lab 5 before the sergeant agreed to accompany her to the equipment tent on the far side of the camp. He'd initially insisted on going alone, but when Nadia explained the technical complexity of what she needed to do, he'd backed down.

I'm not some helpless maiden needing your protection, she'd thought, but kept the sentiment to herself. She did, after all, need the man's flame thrower. Plus, the Kevlar and fatigues del Vega ordered one of his men to surrender to her would help against bat claws.

I hope.

"Okay," del Vega said, his ugly face set with determination. Then he counted down into his radio so Raine could time his flyby accordingly. "Go!"

The Venezuelan ripped open the lab's door and rolled outside. Nadia followed while one of the remaining militiamen resealed it.

The kaleidoscope of sensations that slammed into Nadia was more shocking than she'd expected. While humans could not hear bats ultrasonic echolocation clicks, the din of tens of millions of wings was thunderous. The swirling, miasmic eddies of them dashing, diving, spinning, and wheeling seemed to increase air pressure, as though the enormous mass pressing down on the camp was slowly squeezing it. Then there was the stench of guano, a foul sensation, like someone spraying acid up her nostrils, making her eyes stream and her throat tighten.

A blazing tongue of fire swept above her head, roasting dozens of the tiny mammals and scattering many more. She could hardly see del Vega amidst the swarm, but she thought she heard a manic cackle of enjoyment. But, just then, a new sensation assaulted her as Raine swung his Huey down low above the apex of the lab tent, clearing enough of a path ahead for Nadia to see.

She didn't hesitate.

"Come on!" she barked at del Vega, ducking beneath his spray of flame and grasping his forearm as she dashed past him, racing across the camp.

Raine went first, flying low and dipping his helicopter's nose towards the ground. Unlike their strange kamikaze assault above the sinkhole, the swarm parted before the Huey's passage, opening a corridor for Nadia and del Vega. They charged down it, del Vega letting off sporadic bursts from his flame thrower. Nevertheless, several bats still flung themselves at Nadia, more aggressive than she anticipated, as though sensing her as a threat. As she passed Lab 2, where she hoped King and Sid took shelter, their aggression seemed to increase tenfold. Entire aerial phalanxes broke off from the main army to drive her away.

Don't be ridiculous, she chided herself. She tried to steal a glance through the lab's open door, desperate to see her friends, but the mass was so dense that it was as though a storm cloud had actually settled upon the tent.

"Maybe they're trying to get their mask back," Yousef's comment repeated in Nadia's head.

Indeed, she considered that the bats they had encountered in the tunnels only appeared when they arrived at the Mask Chamber's door. The crocodiles within only attacked King when he found the mask within the niche. And now, after six months without such incident, an undiscovered colony tens of millions strong had only descended on the expedition once they retrieved the mask.

Sid's superstition has been rubbing off on me, Nadia told herself, shaking such nonsensical notions from her head. The only way to save her friends was to complete her mission.

With renewed determination, she bolted away from Lab 2, whirling her arms around her head to knock any attackers aside. Seared flesh added to the stench as del Vega ran after her, flame thrower swirling in fiery arcs. It seemed all Raine could do to keep his helicopter away from it.

Then she skidded to a halt outside another tent, identical to Lab 5. From the outside, the labs, equipment and mess tent all looked like enormous wedding marquees, though now splattered in bat faeces.

Nadia dropped to her hands and knees, opening the door zip just enough so she could squeeze inside.

"Hurry," she shouted to del Vega. He let off a couple of final bursts of fire and slid through the small opening. Nadia resealed the door the moment the Venezuelan was inside, but three bats made it in. They dashed up to the apex, thrashing against the inside of the canvas. An explosion of machine gun fire obliterated them into a fine red mist. The bullets also sliced through the fabric, making Nadia turn to glare at del Vega.

The sergeant lay on the ground, breathing

heavily, a sadistic grin on his face. He flicked chunks of roasted bat from his uniform and rolled to his feet.

Provided by Sharpe Enterprises, the tent was filled with every conceivable piece of equipment that might be required for a scientific expedition of Sarisariñama's scale. From the humble wheelbarrows, mattocks and trowels to state-of-the-art LiDAR setups, digital microscopes, GPS surveying technology and 3D printers, it was the stuff most field archaeologists could only dream of.

"Del Vega, Nadia, you guys okay?" Raine's voice crackled over del Vega's radio.

"We're fine," del Vega barked back. Then, to Nadia, he added, "let's get on with this."

Nadia was already ahead of him, dashing across the tent to the shelving unit at the far end. She glanced through the labels on the Really Useful Boxes before finding the one she needed. Del Vega butted in, helping her pull the RUB down, even though she was more than capable of managing the twenty kilos it weighed. Then she ripped off the lid and extracted one of two yellow cylinders, each about a metre long.

"So, what's the plan again?" del Vega demanded. Nadia shot him a flash of irritation but nevertheless picked up the device and ordered him to follow with a reel of cabling.

"This is a side scan sonar device," she explained, setting it down next to an enormous bank of computer servers, the communications hub of the entire expedition. "We use it in marine archaeology to detect potential underwater anomalies or to map submerged structures. I was thinking we might use it in the chamber we found today," she added. Then she pointed across the other side of the tent. "That toolbox," she said. "Get me a small cross-head screwdriver and wire cutters."

The set of del Vega's jaw warned Nadia that he didn't like being ordered around. Certainly not by a woman. She didn't care. Instead, she hurried to a nearer shelf and retrieved a plastic box filled with computer leads. When they both returned to the sonar device, Nadia quickly unscrewed a metallic side panel and pulled several wires free. Then she retrieved a USB cable from her box and cut the head off, leaving a five-centimetre-long tail which she then stripped.

She continued explaining her plan to del Vega as she worked. "Bats use echolocation to map their surroundings, target their prey and coordinate their flight."

"Because they're blind," del Vega added.

"A common but incorrect belief," Nadia replied. "However, echolocation is arguably their primary 'sense' if you want to correlate it with what we consider senses. Dumbing the science down to something you can understand," she continued, ignoring the militiaman's indignant bristling. "Echolocation works by emitting ultrasonic clicks so high in the sound spectrum that humans cannot hear."

Cutting two wires feeding into the sonar device's inner workings, she reattached them to the decapitated USB head. Once satisfied, she connected the device's newfound USB attachment to an audio decoder plugged into the comms. equipment. Then she stood, opened the server's master laptop and flew her fingers across the keyboard. She noted del Vega trying to keep up with the numerous programmes and tabs she quickly opened and adjusted.

"So, you're tying the sonar device into the camp's comm. equipment," del Vega realised.

Nadia nodded. "If you have a bat infestation in your home or garden, you can buy sonic bat deterrents on Amazon," she explained. "They emit ultrasonic sounds which bats find uncomfortable and avoid," she added. "But, using an industrial side-sonar unit and patching the ultrasonic noise through every emitter on this mountain – conveniently all tied into SharpeSat's network coverage – this should emit a sonic burst powerful enough to force the swarm away." Then she glanced at him, raising an eyebrow and an ever-so-slightly smug grin. "More humane yet effective than a flame thrower, perhaps."

Then she hit ENTER.

"Here goes."

FROM the vantage point he'd returned to after seeing Nadia and del Vega safely inside the equipment tent, Raine watched the incredible spectacle. There was no discernible noise, no announcement, no shock wave or pulse rippling out across the mountain. But he knew the moment Nadia had put her plan into action.

Like a choreographed dance routine, all of a sudden, the black blanket that had descended on the base camp spasmed. Tens of millions of bats lifted into the air, moving as a single entity. They tried to resist the uncomfortable ultrasonic white noise Nadia pumped into the atmosphere, twitching, dipping, diving and swirling.

The spectacle reminded Raine of a lava lamp or sand art. A new mini-landscape was formed each time one upended it, only to be destroyed on the next rotation. Sure enough, the black carpet was one moment a storm-tossed sea, the next a mountainous horizon, a sculpted canyon, or a cloud-speckled skyscape.

And then, unable to resist any longer, the mass broke apart, order collapsed into chaos, and the entire swarm surged away from the camp.

Directly towards him.

"Shit," he cursed, pulling out of his hover. The swarm moved at an incredible pace, its leading edge only seconds away. Knowing that applying the power he needed to roar up and over them would take too long, Raine allowed gravity to give him a helping hand. He pushed down on the collective, sheering to the left and dropping below Sarisariñama's upper lip. Its rocky cliff face screeched past in a blur as Raine spun the Huey about, diving nose first towards the jungle floor, thousands of feet below.

A blanket of darkness fell over him, and he realised that the swarm also dropped down the cliff face as though pursuing one-half of Maria's dreaded Rain King.

I've had enough bats for one day, he thought, applying more thrust to his almost vertical, high-speed descent. The chopper vibrated uncontrollably around him, the cyclic bucking in his grasp. He tore through the cloud cover that ringed the table mountain's summit, the emerald expanse of rainforest now glistening below, growing ever larger as he raced towards it. Then, at the last possible second, he pulled back hard on the collective and twisted the cyclic, his feet working furiously on the antitorque pedals to control the tail rotor. The Huey bucked, the hull seeming to scream a tortured cry, and the engines howled their fury at him, threatening to stall again.

That's when he realised he wouldn't make it. Even as he levelled the Huey's descent, he saw that he would slam the underbelly into the towering tree tops before he was able to climb.

Just need an extra couple of metres, he thought. Then his eyes locked on the reddish-brown swath cutting through the startling green. It was one of the iron-rich tributaries that flowed around Sarisariñama towards the *Rio de Sangre*. Fed by waterfalls tumbling from the cursed mountain itself, the high iron content gave the river its name - Blood River.

Raine altered his pitch and changed the angle of descent just enough so that, as he pulled back on the collective and brought the chopper level, he dropped into the avenue that the river had cut through the trees. The Huey's skids skimmed just above the water, its propellors drawing ripples across its surface.

But he wasn't out of trouble yet. The swarm of

bats had mirrored his flight path, sweeping down the cliff face like a black waterfall and then surging across the treetops, many tens of thousands also dropping into the river channel.

Raine opened the Huey's throttle and powered ahead of the leading edge of the wave, racing down the river's sinuous twists and turns only metres above it. Ahead, it grew narrower, tightening into a bottleneck that was barely wide enough for the circumference of his rotors. He knew all it would take was a single tree branch clawing out over the river to nick his blades and throw him off course, crashing into the jungle. But he held steady, eyes focused on the path ahead. He arched to the left, following a particularly tight river bend, then straightened out as he saw his escape route.

"Come on," he cried, pushing forward harder and faster. The river channel opened up again as it churned towards the top of an enormous waterfall.

The Huey shot over the top, keeping level, the sudden increase in elevation above the treeline giving Raine the freedom to haul back on the collective and work the pedals, banking and gaining altitude.

Below him, the swarm of bats continued its biblical exodus across the rainforest, plunging over the waterfall and spreading across the land, far into the distance.

Raine slowed to a hover and sucked in several deep breaths, mesmerised by the sight. Then, as the morass moved under him, he brought his eyes up, following the line of the river back the way he'd come; back towards the hulking, domineering flat-topped block of stone towering above the jungle.

"You must not go to the Dark Mountain," Maria's voice echoed in his mind.

"Starting to think I should have listened to you," he grumbled, then headed back towards Sarisariñama.

THE LABYRINTH, SARISARIÑAMA TEPUI, VENEZUELA

"I think they're gone," Alverez whispered, terrified of alerting any remaining bats to their presence.

He and Emilio Juan hung from the galvanised cable, suspended from the centre of the gantry arm, just below the level of the tunnel's floor. They were underneath the deluge of bats, yet high enough above the water not to attract the crocodiles.

They hoped.

Their muscles burned from the effort of holding their body weight as millions of bats screeched through the tunnels.

It felt like they had spent eternity in purgatory, trapped between two hells. Juan had prayed the entire time, convinced he had seen the devil standing amidst the cloud of bats in the tunnel. Alverez insisted it was just a trick of the mind, most likely one of the skulls catching his eye. But he supposed a little divine intervention wouldn't hurt.

The deluge of bats finally thinned, becoming nothing but a flitting trickle until the tunnel above their heads was finally motionless again.

Juan's panicked breath plumed around his head as he finished his latest prayer and glowered at his friend. "*Now*, can we get out of here?"

This time, Alverez didn't argue.

25:

UNESCO BASE CAMP, SARISARIÑAMA TEPUI, VENEZUELA

THERE was a strange juxtaposition between the muted stillness within the canvas, coffin-like structure in which King and Sid hid and the manic thrashing of wings and smashing equipment just beyond it.

They lay in a tangle of limbs, King on top of her, their sweaty, dishevelled bodies pressing against one another. It was the most intimate moment the couple had shared for months.

"What the hell was that, Ben?" Sid demanded, getting her breathing under control following her mad dash across the camp.

A giant bat slammed into the fabric wall of the workbench, making them jump.

"What was what?" King asked.

"You? Risking life and limb for that thing? For the second time today," she added, eyes shifting to the mask in her boyfriend's hand.

King glanced at it also, absorbing its twisted façade, the bared teeth and angry eyes, yet finding beauty in it, sensing a thrill pass through his body.

"I couldn't let it get damaged," King explained. "I've finally got the-"

"The proof," Sid cut in. "Yes, I know. But at what cost? If Nate hadn't saved us-"

"Nate?" King scoffed. "Of course, I'm the one who rescues the mask from a crocodile-infested chamber, who makes one of the greatest discoveries in the history of humanity. But Nathan Raine's the hero who gets to swoop in and steal the glory."

"I thought McKinney was the glory-thief," Sid reminded him, shifting her weight under him. "What's your problem with Nate, anyway?"

"What, you mean other than how he swoops in here every fortnight like he owns the place? That he lounges around in the Mess Tent, nursing a bottle of bourbon and looking like the shiftiest man alive? That he has a queue of otherwise respectable, well-educated women practically swooning over him, reduced to little more than mindless Bond girls?"

"Sounds like you're jealous," Sid said.

"Well, he hit on you, didn't he? Back when we met in Caracas?"

King pictured the moment in exact detail. The UNESCO team gathered in a restaurant for a bon voyage meal before shipping to Sarisariñama the following day. Raine had been there, smarming his way through every female present, only Nadia having the sense to send him on his way. Even Sid had seemed mesmerised by the blue-eyed American, with his wry grin, five-o'clock shadow and ruffled black hair.

"Yeah," she admitted. "But he backed off once he realised we were a couple. Not that it was very obvious," she added with a bitter undertone.

A loud crash and clatter of something falling against the workbench shocked them. Still, they were more caught up in their argument than their predicament to give it much consideration.

"What the hell is that supposed to mean?" King asked.

Sid bit back an angry retort, controlling her words. "You know what I mean," she replied, unable to mask the sadness underlining her statement. She felt a pang of guilt for eliciting the look of hurt in her boyfriend's eyes. But it felt good to have finally said the words that had danced on the tip of her tongue for so long.

"We came on this dig to make a new start," she continued. "But it feels like we've been growing more distant since we arrived. And I know that you're still grieving," she added. "But your dad would want you to be happy." Something else clashed outside, sending several bats whirling into the canvas sides of their hiding place. They both ignored it, eyes locked on one another's, faces inches apart.

"Look," Sid whispered. "I think your view of Nate is warped. So, he's a little arrogant," she shrugged, "but he's also a nice guy. He probably saved Karen's life by evacuating her so quickly. As for his *swooning band of Bond-girls* . . . so what? A few young interns, stuck in the middle of the jungle, have a crush on an exciting older man. You've had your fair share of followers on previous digs. That was how *we* got together, remember?"

Sure enough, the memory assaulted King, returning him to the dusty excavation site on the west coast of Crete. In exchange for continued funding, the university had forced him to run a field school for undergraduate students, and Sid, working towards her PhD, had agreed to assist him. Until then, they had known each other professionally. But, whether it was the sun, sea and romantic setting, that they were the only people their own age on the dig or the copious amounts of honey *raki* they drank one evening, one thing had led to another. They had staggered back to his hostel room, lips refusing to part from one another.

In a flash, he relived the moment in exact detail – he could smell the floral scent of her shampoo as he ran his hands through her luscious, jet-black hair. He could feel the smoothness of her skin as his hand drifted down the slender arch of her spine. It slid over her firm buttocks before making the return journey, only this time up the inside of her thigh, underneath the thin material of the summer dress she wore. He could hear her gasp as his fingers found her tender spot, probing softly through the cotton of the flimsy underwear. He felt his heart racing, pumping hot blood through his body to where it needed to be as he watched her wriggle one shoulder out of her dress, then the other, unveiling her caramel flesh, her rounded breasts, nipples hard with excitement-

As though she shared the intensity of the memory, Sid broke through it now by launching herself into a hungry kiss, wrapping her legs around his waist and pulling him to her.

Lying inside a canvas-sided workbench - in a bat-besieged research lab - was as incongruous as a moment of erotism could get. Yet they both surrendered to it, tearing at the other's clothing, lips refusing to part, exploratory fingers eliciting moans and groans of pleasure.

They were lost to the moment, consumed by one another.

Time slowed. King was both aware and yet oblivious to the sensation, just as he had been as he lay trapped underwater that morning. The part of his brain that was aware of it knew it went beyond the cliché of 'time standing still'. Despite its racing, adrenaline-fuelled palpitations, he sensed his heart rate slow; the couple's rapid, exhilarated breathing grew into long, deep breaths. Even the manic thrashing of the bats beyond their canvas hideaway decelerated so much that he heard the distinct *thwump-thwump* of each wing punching the air.

The Moon Mask lay jammed between the canvas and their writhing bodies, as if watching them, leering at them. Each time King's arm brushed the cold metal, a strange warmth permeated through him, a shudder of ecstasy not of Sid's doing.

Without thinking about it, his left hand slipped from his girlfriend's flesh and slid over the contours of the mask. A new wave of pleasure coursed through him, a sense of contentment, fulfilment.

Then he was lost to the moment again, a moment trapped like grains of sand in the neck of an hourglass. He existed both here and now with Sid, yet also in that first intimate encounter with her on Crete; all at once, both vivid, real, yet distant and dreamlike. His girlfriend's hair was simultaneously plastered to her face by the mountain's humidity yet blew wildly in the Cretan breeze coming through the hotel window. Her evening dress lay on the cool tile floor as he lifted her naked onto the bed, yet her dirt-smeared vest and cargo trousers clung and twisted around her sweat-drenched body.

For a moment, he saw the mask on her face as she settled against the hotel room's plush white pillow and within the khaki canvas in the Lab Tent. He recoiled, stepping back from the bed and pushing away within their impromptu love nest. But she pulled him to her, and he was thankful that his lips met her own and not the twisted visage of the mask.

"Sid?" A voice cut through the blood thumping through his ears. "Ben?"

They ignored it for a moment, still caught up in their impromptu tryst, but the memory of Crete faded, and King's hand moved away from the mask.

"Are you in here?" the Russian-accented voice barked, failing to mask Nadia's concern completely.

With great reluctance, Sid and King returned to reality. Chests heaving as they calmed their breathing, their lips reluctantly parted. King noticed that the lab had fallen eerily silent, the crazed bombardment of bats gone.

How long have we been in here? he wondered, disorientated by the time loss.

"We're fine, Nadia," Sid called at last. King looked down at his girlfriend, noting the grin on her face and the sparkle in her eyes. He realised that he hadn't seen either for a long time.

Hastily readjusting their clothes, King unzipped the canvas and peered out. Sid scrambled up next to him.

The lab was in ruins. Smashed glass phials, shattered computer monitors, upended benches and spilt chemicals were everywhere. Most of the bats had fled, only a handful flitting at the apex of the roof, searching for an escape route. Glancing outside, King saw the swarm speed away to the south.

It's over, he thought, but couldn't shake a follow-up sentiment. *For now.*

26:

**HAMARK ASYLUM,
WILLIAMSBURG, VIRGINIA,
BRITISH NORTH AMERICA,**

1727

"**SAVAGE** mumbo-jumbo. Savage mumbo-jumbo. Savage mumbo-jumbo."

"Poor wretch," Johnathon Hawke said as he gazed through the rusted iron bars upon the pitiful form of Edward Pryce. The former slave ship captain sat in his cell, rocking backwards and forwards on the spot.

Far from the severe, handsome man he had once been, Pryce now looked like a creature ripped from the darkest pit of hell.

His once broad shoulders were stooped, and his muscular frame was skeletal. His face was skull-like and terrifying, a disfigured mass of flesh and gristle where his nose had once been. The absence of an upper lip revealed the top row of yellowed teeth. His flesh had partially rotted away, and his scalp was hairless. His skin was broken and puckered by boils and lesions that had long since burst, scabbed and scarred.

Edward Pryce was a monster in every sense of the word.

"Open the door," Hawke ordered.

"But he's dangerous, sir," the guard replied. "Quite mad. Kill us on sight, like as not."

"I have paid your warden for his release. Now," Hawke turned his grey eyes upon the slack-jawed jailer. "Release him."

The guard hesitated a moment longer, then obeyed. A large key turned in the lock, its loud squeal eliciting wild commotion from the other inmates in neighbouring cells. With the raucousness of caged animals, they ran to their cell doors, dirty hands reaching through the bars, inquisitive faces pushing against them, bloodshot eyes peering out at the stranger.

Hawke kept his eyes on Pryce the entire time. The other man didn't so much as flinch.

The big wooden door swung open, and the stench of human waste assaulted Hawke's nostrils. While the guard grimaced, Hawke's face remained expressionless as he pulled a handkerchief from the breast pocket of his silk waistcoat and placed it against his nose.

"Leave us," he told the guard.

The guard looked between the deranged lunatic, rocking back and forth in his cell, and the rather sophisticated gentleman wearing a startling white, expensive-looking suit. While he appeared to be young and well-built, streaks of grey ran through his hair, making him appear older than he was. He carried no weapons that he could see, merely a strange metal box with a handle.

This was not the sort of man, the guard decided, who could hold his own against a trained and savage killer such as Pryce.

Nevertheless, Hawke was not a man used to asking twice.

"Leave us," he snapped. His tone derailed any further thoughts of protest from the guard. The man scuttled away down the long, cold corridor, echoing footsteps lost beneath the wails and catcalls from the other cells.

Hawke stood on the doorway's threshold for a long time, waiting for the excitement in the other cells to calm. Eventually, an eerie silence drifted back into place. It was broken only by the incessant dripping of a nearby leak and the occasional cough and retch from the cells. And, of course, the constant, insane ramblings of the wretched man at which he looked.

Once all was silent, he spoke.

"Edward Pryce," he began. "My name is Hawke. Johnathon Hawke." There was still no reaction, not even a twitch, from the lunatic. But Hawke knew he could hear him, understand him.

"I represent a group of people whose interests intersect with your own."

The very notion of the monstrous-looking inmate having any interests beyond the nest of his own filth in which he sat seemed as crazy as the inhabitants of this damned place.

But Hawke knew better.

He had read Pryce's log from his final transatlantic crossing. He knew about his journey into Africa's dark, savage heart to capture the populous Bouda tribe. Of course, when Pryce's ship was found adrift off the coast of Jamaica two years ago, no one believed the deaths of all but one slave and all of the crew except Pryce resulted from a curse. It was merely some terrible tropical illness.

Along with Pryce's log, an ancient African relic he described as a 'Moon Mask' had ended up in the hands of the young English naval officer who had boarded the *L'aille Raptor*, Percival Lowe. Only when the officer's entire household and the occupants of neighbouring houses had fallen ill and died did anyone pay attention to the heathen mask the slavers brought back with them.

The church became involved, as did the Governor of Jamaica. That is how knowledge of it came to the Grand Master of Hawke's Lodge, comprised of some of the most powerful men in the world. They acquired the mask and log before the church could destroy the heathen idol.

The latter proved invaluable to deciphering the mask's secrets, especially in describing the lead altar in which it had been kept. The Grand Master, who had presided over numerous witch trials at Salem in his younger years, knew of the magical properties of lead. Witches used it because they considered it a 'silent metal'. It could block all forms of energy and create a black space within which to conduct their despised craft unseen. Sure enough, the replica lead-lined altar the Lodge commissioned seemed to contain the mask's power as hoped.

The irony wasn't lost on Hawke: a cabal of men who had condemned women to burn at the stake for witchcraft using that same esoteric knowledge to parade around in ritualistic ceremonies wearing a supposedly magical mask.

The Moon Mask was brought out only on special occasions, to be witnessed exclusively by those sworn into the 33rd Degree of Freemasonry. For a matter of minutes at a time, such limited exposure seemed to control the detrimental effects of the mask's dark magic.

The 33rd Degree was the Golden Law of his Lodge and had been ever since, according to legend, the Founding Fathers had escaped persecution in Ancient Egypt through a 'portal in time'. Time travel was, therefore, central to the Lodge's identity. The Moon Mask's supposed ability to show its wearer future events had, in only two years since the Grand Master had acquired it, cemented its role in the Lodge's mythology as their single, most treasured possession.

And that's what it will remain, he thought. *Just another arcane ancient relic being paraded around by the rich old men of Williamsburg in their egocentric little ritual re-enactments.*

He knew their vaults were full of idols and objects taken from cultures and lands around the world, and their purpose twisted to fit the mythology of the Freemasons.

But the Moon Mask was not just another carving or statue. It contained power. Real power. The sort of power that could further the supposed goal of the Lodge and the so-called great men of Virginia. Right now, that goal was scarcely more than an idea, a dream of independence from British rule, whispered and spoken about behind closed doors. But none, not the Grand Master nor the upper echelons of the Lodge, had the courage to do what needed to be done.

Despite their bold words and protestations, they were content to be ruled.

Hawke was not.

He intended to take control of his future, that of Virginia and any colony brave enough to follow him.

That journey to independence begins now, here in this hellish asylum, facing off against the devil himself.

"I wish to employ your services, Captain Pryce."

Still no response.

"I have procured for you a ship and crew. All they need is a captain."

It was a gamble. A huge one considering he was gambling with a large quantity of the Lodge's money without their consent. Not only had he used it to purchase a ship and crew for Pryce, but also to pay for the madman's release from the asylum.

It was not an insignificant sum.

Hawke's future in the Lodge, possibly his life, hinged on this one-sided conversation with a man the entire world had declared insane.

"I need you to find something for me, Captain

Pryce. Something very precious."

Still nothing.

He went in for the kill.

"The Moon Mask."

Pryce's head snapped around. His eyes focussed on Hawke as though he was the first person he had seen alive since leaving Africa on his ill-fated crossing.

A small smile turned the corner of Hawke's lips upwards. "You know, they say you're insane, Captain Pryce. They say you picked up a tropical disease that wiped out your crew. Watching them die horrifically, even while your own body rotted and withered, sent you mad."

Pryce's face twitched.

"But you and I both know you are anything but insane. Obsessed, perhaps. But not insane. I've read your log- it was coherent throughout. Every single entry, right up until the day the *H.M.S. Swallow* found you adrift."

Now, Pryce had returned to his previous state, but Hawke could tell that it took all his mental self-control to remain that way.

"You watched and recorded in your log the hideous, excruciating death of every man aboard the *L'aille Raptor*. You recorded every detail, *every exact detail* logically, coolly, just as you recorded every event before the curse struck you.

"No, Captain Pryce," Hawke continued without interruption. "I do not believe you are insane. I think you are a fraud. A coward!"

There was emotion there, deep in those dark, beady eyes. Anger.

"Even with your crew dead, you did what you could to ensure the *Raptor* made her crossing. That she made it to landfall somewhere in the New World . . . so that you could abandon her. Then what? Escape into the wilderness, live off the land?

"But the *Swallow* found you first. You knew your patrons, the Lewison brothers – a rather unsavoury pair of brutes to do business with if you would like my opinion - would kill you for your ineptitude. You lost your whole crew and your entire cargo . . . their entire investment in your enterprise. If they knew you survived, they wouldn't stop hunting you down. I dare say, your death would likely have been slower, more painful and altogether more unpleasant than that of your crew."

Pryce was still playing dumb, trying to look vacant. But Hawke could see the intelligence behind those eyes. The cunning.

"So, where could a disfigured, bankrupt slave trader find safety in any form? Who would give him charity? Mercy?" He looked about at his surroundings, curling his nose.

Any other man might have quit there and then, the lifeless stare of the former slaver empty, disinterested. But Hawke saw the flash of concern: he was a good actor, but not good enough.

"Still nothing, Captain?" he pressed, shrugging and turning to leave. "Very well. Perhaps I shall run my 'theory' by the warden. Reveal you as a fraud, milking him and his establishment all these years. Reveal your cowardice-"

Pryce moved as quick as a flash.

Unfurling himself from his nest of filth, he lunged at Hawke. His eyes blazed, his hideous face contorted with rage.

He reached out with his hands, ready to wrap them around Hawke's throat, squeeze the life from him, and bash his head against the ground.

Dead men tell no tales, Hawke mused, even as he responded just as quickly as the captain.

Anticipating Pryce's reaction, he spun on his heel, ripping out the only weapon he carried.

The Moon Mask.

27:

UNESCO BASE CAMP, SARISARIÑAMA TEPUI, VENEZUELA

"**ARE** you okay?" Nadia demanded as King and Sid emerged into the sunlight.

"We're fine, Nadia," Sid said, taking King's hand as they scrambled from their canvas hideaway and stepped out of the lab into the sunlight. The other expedition personnel staggered through the ruins of the camp.

"Is everyone else?"

"With you two accounted for, yes," the Russian replied.

Raine's helicopter swooped overhead and

circled the landing site in the neighbouring clearing. Clutching the Moon Mask, King watched it slow to a hover, preparing to land.

He surveyed the damaged camp, amazed at the destruction the bats had wrought. Their combined mass had ripped guy-ropes from the ground, scattering tents and their contents everywhere. Clothes, books and toiletries were strewn across the mountain top, along with food and rubbish from the upturned waste bins. They had even demolished one of the compost toilets beneath their combined weight. To make matters worse, everything was coated in bat guano, the acrid stench stinging King's eyes.

A sudden hiss startled him, drawing his attention to a fire near the Mess Tent. Two Ye'kuana workers threw a bucket of water over a campfire that had spread out of control during the chaos. They quickly took command of the small blaze, but King's eyes nevertheless fixed onto the remaining flames. He watched them dance, swaying hypnotically, sensually even. The sounds of the camp grew distant, the crackling of embers and the hiss-pop of vaporising water consuming him.

The flames filled his entire vision, their roar beating like tribal drums in his head. He struggled to breathe as a face swirled through the smoke: the Moon Mask. But then it was gone, replaced by another visage and, for just a moment, a terrible moment, he thought it was his father burning, screaming in agony-

"Watch it, Benny. You trying to singe your eyebrows or something?"

The voice snapped him back to the moment, the flames extinguished under another bucket of water. The steam hissed like a nest of vipers, making him jump. The Ye'kuana men glanced at him, puzzled by his presence. He realised he was kneeling in front of the now smouldering firepit, having walked across the entire camp. Only, he didn't remember taking a single step.

He glanced up at the man who had spoken- dark, dishevelled hair, stubbled chin, piercing blue eyes. He swallowed his instinctual dislike, wondering how Raine had managed to land and secure his helicopter and make it to the base camp so quickly. He had just been hovering above the landing site mere seconds ago.

"McKinney told me you'd smacked your head over the radio," Raine said, seeming to adjust his clothing as though he'd only recently dressed. "I didn't realise it was this bad."

"Ben?" Sid asked before he could respond to the American. Behind his girlfriend, he noticed that several upturned tents had been righted, guy ropes tied down. Yet he had no memory of any of that happening; one moment, he was outside Lab 2 with Sid and Nadia, the next, he was kneeling by the fire outside the Mess Tent.

A wave of panic swept through him. That was the second block of time that was missing from his memory. He could explain the first by the intensity of his intimate liaison with Sid. He'd merely lost track of time, not noticing the bats depart the tent and the base return to normality. But this? This made no sense to him.

Maybe the concussion really is worse than I thought.

Sensing his distress, Sid grasped his arm, looking askance. But Raine was oblivious, glancing instead at what he held in his hand.

"So, this is it, huh? What's got all you history nerds in a frenzy," Raine said. There was something intense behind his grin, however. Something somehow dangerous. "About time you guys earned your keep. Can I see it?"

The American reached for the mask in King's hand, but the archaeologist snatched it away, cradling it. An explosion of anger replaced his previous sense of panic.

"No," he barked at Raine, glaring at him. Then, realising his over-reaction, he took a breath and forced an explanation. "It's . . . it's really fragile."

Raine raised a quizzical, if slightly amused

eyebrow, no doubt about to make some wisecrack about how he was handling the precious object. But McKinney's voice cut him off, the Glaswegian booming across the base camp.

"All right, everybody!" She clapped her hands to catch the entire team's attention. Nadia ignored her as she approached the trio, opening a secure, padded container and offering it to King.

For the mask, he realised, suddenly apprehensive about letting it go.

You're being ridiculous, he chided himself. *What the hell has gotten into you?*

He placed the mask inside the container and forced himself to look away as Nadia snapped it shut. He gasped as though shouldering a grievous loss.

"There is a large storm-front due to hit us tomorrow morning," McKinney announced. "And we've already wasted too much time today." She shot an accusing glance in King's direction, but he ignored it. "I'm calling a halt to all excavation work until the storm passes. I want one member from each team up here, getting basecamp back up and running. The rest need to get back into the tunnels to secure any equipment and finish any recording before the flood hits. I'll be proceeding with the plan to retrieve the human remains from the chamber we found this morning."

She softened her voice ever-so-slightly. "I know that, after what just happened, all any of us want is to crack open a crate of beer. I promise you, with no tunnel work tomorrow, we can go crazy tonight. But, until then, I need everyone on top form . . . and to do *exactly* as I say."

"Was she looking at you then?" Raine asked King.

When King didn't reply, Sid answered for him. "Maybe," she admitted.

"Come on, people, move!" the expedition leader barked, clapping her hands and corralling the team into action.

Nadia raised an eyebrow. "Definitely," she added.

"Doctor Yashina, Mister Raine," McKinney turned to them. "Let's go."

Nadia shot her friends an apologetic look as she followed McKinney, but Raine looked confused.

"Aren't you coming, Benny?" he asked. "This is your big discovery, isn't it?"

King's eyes shifted from McKinney's retreating figure to Raine's obnoxious face, but Sid cut in again before he could reply.

"We're sitting this one out," she explained. Then, on Raine's askance expression, she added, "It's a long story."

King felt suddenly conscious of the intensity of Raine's stare, his icy eyes betraying the casual demeanour he sought to project.

Why the hell does he care whether I'm on the excavation team or not? he wondered.

The intense flash in the American's eyes vanished as quickly as it had appeared, but it left King unsettled. Raine may have had Sid and everyone else fooled with his cocky grin as he shrugged, said he'd see them later, and then swaggered away, but King wasn't buying it.

"Just remember," Sid said, mistaking the tautness of his body for a resurfacing of jealousy. "I'd much rather have the all-American action hero get eaten by crocs than the man I love."

But, after their intimate tryst, her boyfriend's response wasn't what she had hoped.

"I've got to get into the tunnels."

28:

HAMARK ASYLUM, WILLIAMSBURG, VIRGINIA, BRITISH NORTH AMERICA,

1727

HAWKE held the Moon Mask out before him like a shield.

The moment Pryce laid eyes on it, he panicked, his attack faltering.

Staggering backwards, away from the object that had thrust such a terrible affliction upon him, Pryce back-peddled into the far corner of the cell, anger replaced by terror on his monstrous face.

"No," he stammered, holding his hands before his face to shield himself from the mask's dark magic.

It was the first time Pryce had seen it, Hawke

knew, since the *Swallow* had come across him two years ago. And, while not the lunatic he presented himself as, his encounter with the mask had scarred him deeper than just the flesh.

"You'll kill us," Pryce gasped, his throat dry, his voice raw and husky. These were the only words, save for his repetitive mantra, that he had uttered in two years. "You'll kill us both."

Hawke stepped deeper into the cell, closer to the other man. Pryce had nowhere to go and all but whimpered like a beaten dog in the corner.

"If some savage Negro witch doctor can control the mask," he replied, "I most certainly can."

Pryce's eyes did not move from the mask. They took it all in; the beauty of its beadwork, the artistry of the carving, the expert blending of metal and wood. The mask's face was benevolent, soft, warm and colourful. Yet one could not ignore its power nor forget the horrors it had inflicted.

Hawke had seen the same mixture of awe and reverence, fear and disgust, on the faces of poppy addicts.

Pryce at once loathed the cursed thing and yet loved it. He had felt its dark touch, the tickling of the corners of his consciousness, the flashes of memory brought forward by its time-warping magic.

Hawke had felt it also and did so now that he

had unleashed it from its metal case. Even though he wore thick leather gloves to prevent his flesh from encountering it, he could feel its magic invading his mind, bringing forth memories of his younger days, his youth-

"What do you want of me?" Pryce's voice snapped him back to the here and now.

Hawke regained his composure and set forth his simple request. "I want you to find the Moon Mask for me."

Pryce's eyes narrowed, his snarled response scarcely above a whisper. Still, he stared at the mask as though it was a lover who had betrayed him.

"You already have it."

"Part of it," Hawke said, lowering his voice also. It was as though the mask demanded such reverence. "Part of it," he repeated, referring to the metal section that had been expertly incorporated into what was otherwise a simple, if beautiful, African mask. The 'base' of the mask was no different to the hundreds of similar curios that explorers and missionaries collected from the uncivilised lands of the world.

But that one metal section, incorporating an eye and part of the nose, was something else. Something special.

Something magical.

"I want it all."

Pryce understood. *Seeing* through time wasn't enough for Jonathon Hawke: he wanted to *control* it.

"Why me?"

"Because, Captain Pryce," he said, returning to his usual arrogant tone. "You are the only man I know of who has come into direct, prolonged exposure to the Moon Mask's magic . . . and survived. How and why this is, I do not care. All I care about is that such a 'resistance,' if you will, to the curse, makes you uniquely qualified to find the rest of it."

Pryce seemed to take this information in his stride. If anything, the revelation of his 'uniqueness' empowered him, straightening his shoulders and returning confidence to his ugly, distorted face.

"And why should I help you?" he demanded.

"Because, Captain, if you bring me the power to control the future, I will give you the power to change the past." Pryce's eyes locked onto his, dark and probing, as though seeing him for the first time.

"That's right," Hawke pressed. "You, better than anyone, understand the mask's power. You know the Bouda legend is true. The man who controls the mask, the entire, original mask, broken apart by some ancient power and scattered across God's earth, controls the power of time itself. Give me that power," he concluded, "and I will undo . . . this," he waved his hand across Pryce's horrific disfigurement. "I will make you a man again. A great, wealthy . . . *powerful* man." He paused, allowing his words to sink in. "What say you?"

There was a long, dark silence as Pryce stared at him, and it was all Hawke could do to stop him from averting his own eyes from the monster. But then, very slowly, Captain Edward Pryce nodded his head. The raw, red muscles around his lip-less mouth pulled back into the most terrifying smile that Hawke had ever seen.

To win the independence he so desired, Jonathon Hawke realised he had just sold his soul to the devil.

29:

UNKNOWN LOCATION

"ZULU One, I've got an update for you," the man in the yellow tie said into his phone.

Zulu One's response was crisp and direct. *"Go."*

"The target is confirmed: you're looking for this mask." He sent the image file via a secure direct transfer link to Zulu One's device. He didn't know what device the man used – a smartphone, tablet, PC? Nor did he care. He simply knew that he was opening this image. Despite his professionalism, the man in the yellow tie was sure Zulu One's face would be a picture of surprise. His own had been the same when he saw the image posted on one of the Sarisariñama expedition members' social media feeds. The accompanying caption read simply: 'I've found it.'

After overcoming his surprise that something so archaic as the mask depicted in the photo could be so powerful, he'd struggled to contain his amusement at the post's author.

This Benjamin King actually seems to think he knows what he's found, he'd thought. *He doesn't have a clue.*

Zulu One did not acknowledge his surprise or discuss it. There was no comment like 'that's what's caused all this fuss?' or 'I can't believe something like that could be worth risking all-out war over.' Zulu One wasn't about to waste time with such pointlessness. He knew the stakes and the urgency of the situation.

The man in the yellow tie was surprised, therefore, when the voice on the other end of the call raised a concern.

"The Teddy Order, sir?"

The man in the yellow tie didn't deign to sigh. Zulu One knew his silence was enough to convey his displeasure at having his orders questioned.

Zulu One hesitated. Not a common occurrence, the man in the yellow tie knew.

"There are US citizens down there. Personnel from friendly countries. Allies."

The man in the yellow tie knew that the lack of

questions was question enough. His instinctual response was to snap at Zulu One's insubordination. The man knew what was at stake, the cost of failure, the importance of secrecy. All evidence of what the scientists had found at Sarisariñama had to be eradicated. But, as he opened his mouth to snap out the rebuke, he remembered who Zulu One was, the vow he had taken. A vow to protect the United States of America against any and all threats at any and all cost. He would do what needed doing. Still, the Teddy Order against so many innocent American nationals would haunt him forever.

A Teddy Order. What a ridiculous term, the man in the yellow tie thought. He didn't know its origins. Originally it was simply a Terminate Order, later shortened to a T-Order. Somewhere along the line, however, the T had become Teddy. Perhaps named after a person? An incident? Maybe nothing more than a way of softening such a harsh term, humanising such a vile act.

A Terminate Order, after all, was a succinct, clinical way of ordering a scorched earth policy. It was a 'leave no witnesses' cliché, a 'kill every living thing and destroy all evidence of your presence' mandate. It was an easy enough order to follow when taking out an ISIL cell or assassinating an enemy state's leader. It was quite another when butchering the innocent men and women one had sworn to protect.

But the needs of the many, the man in the yellow tie thought. Then, in a rare display of sympathy, he offered Zulu One some small measure of solace to ease the darkness that would engulf him after committing the atrocity.

"You've read the briefing," he said. "If anyone is alive by the time you get there, they'll either be begging for death . . . or so insane that putting them down will be the kindest thing."

Zulu One's silence made the man in the yellow tie feel the need to elaborate.

"It's subtle at first," he continued, his voice dropping to a whisper. He pictured the grainy black and white video footage that had set him on this path. "It starts as intense daydreams of sorts, as though you are reliving a past moment in the most vivid detail. Then it becomes a . . . an infatuation, a lust. Eventually, an obsession. A hunger for the mask, an insatiable thirst."

Indeed, he now knew that hunger for the mask's power went beyond the human brain, affecting animals - mammals and, it seemed, reptiles. He had seen the Adventure Channel's social media updates. He had read the brief UN reports written by the expedition leader. Crocodiles inside the 'Mask Chamber' had been lethargic, only becoming aggressive when the mask was disturbed. And now, the newest update stated that an enormous swarm of bats had seemingly assaulted the camp.

They want the mask, he knew. *They* need *the mask.*

The scientists at Sarisariñama hadn't worked it out yet, but he had. He had seen the recordings of once-rational human beings succumbing to primal instincts. He'd seen them entrapped by a single-minded lust for what the mask offered, tearing one another apart in their desperation to claim it for themselves. Some had even killed themselves when parted from its invisible allure.

"That hunger leads you over the edge of reason," the man in the yellow tie continued. "The daydreams become hallucinations. The hallucinations begin to take over, guiding you down a path into darkness. Darkness from which there is no return." He paused, staring into space, forcing the recordings of those wretched souls out of his head. "So you see, if anyone is still alive when you get there, you'll be doing them a favour."

Zulu One took a breath. Let it go. *"Understood,"* he snapped off. *"We'll take care of it. Wheels up in five."*

Then the man in the yellow tie did something he rarely did. He wished Zulu One and his team good luck. But, as he hung up, one final thought teased his mind.

You'll need it.

30:

UNESCO BASE CAMP, SARISARIÑAMA TEPUI, VENEZUELA

NATHAN Raine wasn't a man easily prone to worry. He was a man of action who threw himself into a situation, confident that his resourcefulness, ingenuity, and cunning would get him out of it in one piece.

Yet, as he marched across the Sarisariñama base camp, he couldn't throw off a sense of dread.

He had always prided himself on an almost sixth-sense-like ability to detect danger before it struck. It wasn't any sort of cliché, like the hair on the back of his neck standing on end or a shiver as some futuristic midnight trespasser supposedly walked over his grave. Nor even so-called butterflies of nerves in his belly.

This ability wasn't something he often consciously considered. Usually, he forgot about it until such time as it made its presence known again. When he did think about it, he often likened it to the stories he had heard of the terrible Boxing Day tsunami in Thailand. There, elephants, dogs, birds, and even herds of buffalo panicked and bolted for high ground long before humans had any sense of peril looming down on them.

That was what he felt now — an urge to turn, to flee something dark and deadly rising like a wave to drown him.

But, whereas animals surrendered to instinct, humans, he mused, often ignore it. As he did now. Indeed, it was Nathan Raine's very nature to hurl himself into the face of danger.

He met the rest of the team by the lift. A noisy generator powered a thick cable through pulleys and wheels. It could lower a basic, open-topped metal cage down to the sinkhole's floor where some expedition teams had worked over the past few months. The contraption looked like some metallic beast crawling from the mist-shrouded depths, at striking odds with the lush vegetation clinging to the sinkhole's sides.

"Hey kids, who's up for an excursion today?" He greeted his companions with mock-cheeriness.

Nadia offered a curt nod in greeting, ignoring his words. Juan and Alverez, the former looking decidedly nervous, broke off a whispered conversation and muttered a hello. However, Raphael del Vega, their boss, merely grunted then walked away, returning his attention to his beloved flame thrower.

"Well, this'll be fun," Raine grumbled at the lack of enthusiasm. Then, in the awkward silence, he tuned into Juan and Alverez's continued conversation.

"I'm just saying, it's . . . funky," Juan said in Spanish.

"Funky?" Alverez repeated. "What's 'funky' is that we've only just got out of that stinking hole and the boss is sending us back down straight away. I'm telling you, it's punishment for losing the drone."

But Juan didn't seem to hear his comrade's words. His gaze shifted to the sinkhole, the beads of sweat pouring down his face betraying his fear.

"No," he mumbled. "I mean it's *funky*," he stressed. "You know, weird, strange, off. A blood-drenched, skull-lined corridor. A secret chamber filled with man-eating crocodiles and venerated human remains."

"They're archaeologists," Alverez argued. "That's what they're here to do." Despite the increasing volume of their voices, the two militiamen apparently felt their conversation in Spanish remained private. Raine, however, was fluent, and he suspected that Nadia was too.

He noticed several cuts on both men's faces and arms, the stench of TCP and smears of antiseptic cream the only evidence of medical treatment. He agreed with their assessment: del Vega was punishing them.

"But don't you think it's strange," Juan pressed his comrade, "that the same day they find some pagan relic, bats attack the camp. I tell you, it is like they are the denizens of the devil." Then he brought a crucifix out from beneath his sweat-stained uniform tunic and kissed it.

"It's just a coincidence, guys," Raine cut in, revealing his grasp of the Venezuelans' predominant language.

Juan's eyes fixed on his, intense. "No, *compadre*," he said, dropping his voice to a whisper. He nodded his head in the direction of the camp. "Everybody is talking about it. About how strange it is that all those bats converged on the lab where they were storing the mask."

He stepped closer to Raine, invading his personal space. TCP mixed with B.O. to blend an unpleasant cologne. The militiaman dropped his voice to a conspiratorial level. "It is like they were searching for it. For what we have stolen from their dark master. I tell you, the Devil walks on this mountain, in these tunnels."

Raine held Juan's gaze for several long seconds, then glanced at Nadia. She had averted her eyes, seemingly disinterested in such superstition.

"What about you, Big Guy?" he called to del Vega as he finished his impatient pacing and returned to them. The powerfully built militia sergeant screwed his face up at Raine's naming convention. But then his visage twisted into a wicked grin, making his cartoonishly large, drooping moustache look even more incongruous on his scarred face.

"If the Devil lives here," he rumbled, patting his flame thrower, "I look forward to meeting him."

Just then, McKinney appeared, hurrying to the lift.

"Oh, thank god," Raine heard Nadia hiss, relieved to escape the conversation. But Raine froze when he saw the camera operator trailing the expedition leader. He stepped up to her just as the Scot spoke to the winch operator, another of the militiamen.

"You are not to let Doctor King down to the tunnels," she told the man.

"I know, I know," the guard replied. "The

Sargento already told me, *senora*. He tried about ten minutes ago. Said he had to retrieve important equipment, but I told him to piss off."

Despite bristling at being called *senora*, the guard's response seemed to be what McKinney wanted to hear. "Very good," she said, but Raine grasped her arm and took her to one side before she could move. "What the hell-"

"You said there'd be no cameras involved," he hissed at her, glancing back at the camera operator who had followed her.

"No, I said you wouldn't be on camera," she argued. "There's a difference."

"My contract explicitly-"

"I know what your contract says, Mister Raine," she cut him off. "And I assure you, the operator is under strict instructions not to film you. Any shots that might catch you in the background will be blurred. And, as per your agreement with Sharpe Enterprises and The Adventure Channel, you'll get to see anything before it is broadcast."

Raine didn't respond for several seconds, weighing up his options. Kira Sharpe herself had talked him into taking this job. He had been reluctant at first due to the high-profile nature of the expedition, but the billionaire entrepreneur was very persuasive. She had assured him that he would be left out of any footage and his name omitted from any records. He worked for Sharpe Enterprises, not UNESCO.

He still wasn't sure why she had insisted that he join the expedition. Returning a favour, she had said, after saving her life: a life for a life . . . or a fresh start anyway.

"Nathan, we need you down there," McKinney said, flashing him a smile. "*I* need you down there. Sharpe told me you'd come in handy when . . . we needed a delicate hand."

Raine tried not to shudder at the older woman's attempt at flirtation.

"Using del Vega and his goons to retrieve fragile human remains on a strict timetable is like using a machete to perform brain surgery. But this is the first thing of note we've found here. The *only* thing," she added. "Adventure Channel needs their pound of flesh, or all our funding will dry up."

Raine sighed. "Okay, but keep that thing out of my face," he said, indicating the camera.

"Of course," she smiled. "Thank you. But, I'm curious, why are you so keen to hide-"

"I like to keep things . . . *private*," he cut her off, adding enough innuendo into the last word to appeal to her flirtatiousness and knock out her line of inquiry. Before she could recover, he waved his hand at the lift with a flamboyant flourish. "Your chariot awaits,

Professor."

The Glaswegian composed herself and brushed past him as she took her place on the lift. Raine was the last one on, turning to glance across the basecamp.

Despite the brilliance of the midday sun slanting through the clearing, that sense of dark foreboding returned.

It's just a coincidence, he had said to Juan. But Raine had enough life experience to be wary of coincidences. He could shrug off Maria's insane warning about the 'Rain King' – just a coincidence for sure. The prophecy of the Evil Spirit manifesting itself in the form of a fanged face? The twisted visage of the mask he had seen King holding? The similarity between his vision of inky blackness flooding the land and the blanket of bats swarming from the mountain? And, try as he might to apply logic to what he saw, Juan's words rang true. Hovering in the Huey above the chaos below, the loops and curls of the bats' flight did indeed seem somehow structured, as though they were fixated on a single goal: finding something.

The Moon Mask?

Get a hold of yourself, Nate, he admonished himself. *Whatever the hell Maria drugged you with last night, it was more potent than I realised.*

With that final attempt at justifying his sudden

bout of superstition, the lift began its descent into the shadows below.

31

UNESCO BASE CAMP, SARISARIÑAMA TEPUI, VENEZUELA

BENJAMIN King clung to the underside of the lift cage as it dropped down the mist-shrouded throat of the Sima Humboldt.

With his knees wrapped around one side of the cage's frame and his elbows around the other, he glanced up through the crisscrossing metal slats at the soles of the retrieval team's boots.

All it would take was for one of the lift's occupants to glance down, and his ruse would be up. Then how would he explain what he was doing? They all thought he was crazy anyway, and he was just proving to them and himself that they were right.

She's making me do this, he told himself, glaring up at McKinney. *I should be the one rescuing Kha'um's remains.*

A rescue, he realised, was exactly what it was.

He couldn't explain it. He just knew that something would happen if he weren't down there with them. Something bad.

I can't let anything happen to Kha'um, he vowed. *This is it. My only chance to justify my entire life. My last chance.*

He couldn't shake the image of the face he had seen in the fire.

A hallucination, he kept telling himself. *A result of your concussion.*

It wasn't his father's face. Or his own. But it felt familiar. *Familial.*

Kha'um. A distant ancestor. A man bound to the Moon Mask in life and in death.

Glancing at the drop below him, he realised how similar their fates could quickly become.

Of course, he had tried the rational approach, joining some other teams heading into the tunnels to batten the hatches before the storm. But the militiaman on duty at the winch had stopped him. After a heated exchange, Sid had convinced him that arguing was pointless.

"Just come back and start work on the mask," she had told him. "Unless you're planning on doing something crazy like abseiling down there, they're not going to let you near the tunnels. I'm sorry." She had led him away from the lift, back into the camp.

"I'll join the guys clearing this place up," she had continued. "You go and start work on the mask. You said something about constructing a 3D printout, didn't you, so you can handle a replica without damaging the original?"

"Yeah," he'd replied half-heartedly, despite his eagerness to see the mask again. "Jiao said she'd help me with it." The Chinese post-graduate student specialised in Digital Archaeology and had developed a specialised scanning program that created exact coloured recreations of archaeological materials.

"Great," Sid had said. "And don't worry- Nadia is the most methodical person I know. She'll look after the human remains properly."

King had flashed her a small smile and watched as she headed off to help with the clean-up. Then he'd turned and looked back at the sinkhole.

Thick, unyielding vegetation choked its walls. Abseiling down really would be crazy. Climbing might be possible but equally hazardous.

No, he'd realised. The lift was the only way in and out of the Labyrinth.

That was when he'd hatched his plan. Though, admittedly, it was more of a knee-jerk reaction than a plan, per se.

He'd made his way to the sinkhole's edge, behind the equipment tent. The lift sat waiting for McKinney and her disciples about 15 metres around the natural curve of the sinkhole's rim.

Confident no one was looking, he climbed into the expanse, clinging to the thickest roots and vines. Though they acted as a natural latticework, making his way around the sinkhole to the lift was harder going than he'd anticipated. Then, trying not to look down, he'd clamoured over the framework, bolted into the cliff face, and found his anchorage points under the lift.

Now, his shoulders and hips throbbed as he tensed them to hold his weight. The metal dug into the underside of his knees and elbows.

He knew from experience that the lift cage's descent was slow. But, as his exhaustion grew with each passing second, it felt painfully so. The thickets of crusted plant growth ambled by, pruned back by the contraption's regular passage.

Then, the moment he had been dreading came.

The sinkhole was wider at the base than at the top. While the lift's scaffolding guided it down two-thirds of the way to the metal platform erected outside the Labyrinth's doorway, the final third was a free fall.

The cage swung free, dangling above the yawning drop below. This was the bit Sid hated every time they made their way to and from the tunnel, clamping her eyes shut and squeezing his hand tight. It had never bothered him.

Until now.

The sensation of the slight swing as it dropped free was minimal to the passengers in the cage. However, gripping its underside, it felt like a swinging pendulum, and the motion dislodged his knees.

His legs dropped from their perch, swinging his entire body vertical and forcing his arms to unwrap from the framework. He grasped it with a single hand, and it was all he could do to keep from crying out.

The fingers of his right hand now took all his weight, the rough edges of the metal bar cutting into the flesh, adding blood to the sweat that already threatened to slide him free.

Shout for help! his mind screamed.

Instead, he heaved his left arm up and grasped the framework. The fire in his right shoulder died only a little, but his sudden movement rocked the cage. Its occupants staggered, and he knew that any second now, one of them would look down-

"Ding!" Raine exclaimed. "Welcome to the Penthouse Level. I do hope you enjoy your stay."

Despite his situation, King took a small amount of satisfaction from the lack of laughter at the American's attempt at humour as they arrived alongside the Labyrinth's doorway. Del Vega grasped a metal chain bolted into the cliff face, holding the lift steady while the others disembarked.

"Come on, come on," King hissed through gritted teeth. His entire body sent waves of pain to his brain as he hung there, trying not to move, trying even harder not to let go.

Del Vega followed the others into the tunnel, and King felt a wave of relief turn to horror as they stopped just inside. In her usual manner, McKinney decided to repeat everything she had told her companions about the importance of their task and the sensitivity of the material they were recovering.

"Move," King growled beneath his breath. His arms trembled. His fingers grew numb. Sweat poured into his eyes, stinging them.

"Right, let's move!" the despised Glaswegian accent barked.

King couldn't hold on any longer. He shifted his weight, trying to haul himself up-

The lift jolted into motion again, the operator reversing the winch to haul it back up.

"Shit!" King cursed as the unexpected motion slammed his body's weight back down, wrenching his shoulder sockets so violently that he let go of the underside of the cage.

He dropped into oblivion-

Then slammed into the platform outside the doorway, the lift rising just above it. The wind exploded out of his lungs, and he slid backwards, his legs still dangling over the void until he jammed his fingers into the metal grating. He felt skin tear and feared his digits would each snap like twigs. But, somehow, they held and arrested his fall.

With a final burst of energy, he heaved himself onto the platform and lay there gasping. The lift cage receded into the heights of the sinkhole, distorting from view behind a veil of silvery mist. It drew across the chasm like a curtain drawn across a stage. For just a moment, a shaft of sunlight broke through. Then, like the last ray of hope being extinguished, the mist curled around it, strangling it into nothing but a muted haze, far from reach.

Benjamin King suppressed the chill that snaked down his spine and rolled to his feet. As he had done countless times over the last six months, he headed through the maw of the tunnel entrance, vanishing into the darkness of the labyrinth within.

Only, this time, something felt different.
Colder.
Darker.

A hushed voice seemed to carry a single word upon the air.
Sari . . . Sari. . .

EPILOGUE: THREADS

. . . **"OKAY,** target's confirmed. Ops gave us the green light." Despite the vocal receptor taped to his throat, transmitting his voice to the radio earpieces each of his team wore, Lawrence Gibbs still shouted above the engines' din.

The plane's hold was dark, his comrades' faces aglow with nothing but dim red light, giving them a demonic persona. The thunder of the large engines echoed through the cold, cavernous space as, in the cockpit, Sykes and Lake made final preparations for take-off.

"Designation confirmed, Boss?" West asked.

Gibbs glanced at the New Yorker, then swept

his gaze across his entire team. "Confirmed," he said. "Code Black."

"I don't get it," Garcia admitted. "A Code Black designation is for clear, immediate WMD threat against the US. How can we have a Code Black in the middle of the Amazon fucking rainforest?"

"We do," Gibbs cut in before anyone commented further. "Simple as that-"

"Uhh, Boss," Lake's voice cut over his earpiece from her seat in the cockpit. *"Might wanna take a look out the port window."*

Gibbs scowled, about to order her to quit the cryptic crap. But, without speaking, he clambered over the equipment stashed along the port side of the hold. Looking down at the runway, the midday glare bouncing off the tarmac, he recognised Rudy O'Rourke's silhouette.

Gibbs then did something rare.

He smiled . . .

. . . **WITH** a rumble of giant motors, the ramp thumped closed behind Rudy O'Rourke. A chorus of cheers welcomed him on board.

"Glad you could make it," West said.

"Thought you was gonna pussy off and leave us to it," Murry added.

"Couldn't let you have all the fun," O'Rourke shot back. Then he glanced at Gibbs, who gave him a firm nod and returned to his seat. O'Rourke buckled himself in next to the team leader and donned a headset in time to hear Sykes' voice report they had clearance for take-off.

"No collateral," O'Rourke rumbled, remembering the Boss's earlier promise.

Gibbs' black eyes speared into him, his face unreadable. "No collateral," he repeated. Then, to Sykes in the cockpit, he barked, "let's go!"

Sykes acknowledged. *"Copy that Zulu One..."*

. . . **HEY** baby, how's it going . . ." Sid's voice trailed off as she pushed through Lab 5's door to find Jiao working alone. The mask lay cushioned in a protective case on a workbench, high-tech instruments Sid assumed were laser scanners slowly moving up its monstrous features.

Jiao turned to her with a smile, but Sid ignored her greeting. A knot tightened itself in her gut as she looked about.

"Where's Ben?"...

. . . **DOCTOR** Burke stood at the foot of the

patient's bed, trying to choke back the rising tide of resentment she felt. She still knew nothing about the woman lying there. That she had contracted some terrible disease was evident from her symptoms. Yet, there was no sign of a foreign body in her system. All her blood works were negative; every scan she and her colleagues had conducted found nothing that could cause what Burke was seeing.

Yet, here she was, lying at death's door, and the only option Burke had left was to follow the advice of a retired radiologist.

She had redirected her initial anger at Emmett Braun to the government goons who had muscled him into the situation. The notes he had hastily scrawled onto the patient's notes were evidently written on the sly. It was Braun's attempt at covertly helping her, she knew.

Burke glanced at them again now.

Diethylenetriamine pentaacetate, Mifepristone, Ketoconazole and Metyrapone.

It made no sense. Mifepristone was commonly used to abort pregnancy, Ketoconazole and Metyrapone were cortisol inhibitors, and Diethylenetriamine pentaacetate treated acute radiation sickness. But, as she had insisted time and again, Burke had detected no radioactive elements in the patient's body.

Now, however, Burke and Patient JH28791 were out of options.

Taking a breath, she attached the medicine bag containing the odd cocktail of drugs to the patient's drip and opened the valve. As she did so, she looked down at the young woman's face, noting the manic twitching of her eyelids again, as though her mind was locked in a perpetual nightmare.

"Who are you?" she whispered . . .

. . . **"WE** have only tapped into the merest fragment of the power of the human brain," Henri Moreau told his lecture hall of bored-looking students. "I'm not talking about the debunked myth that we only use 10 per cent of it. I'll leave that crap to X-Men movies. But, while we use most of it most of the time, we don't use it to its fullest potential.

"Think of it like a Porsche winding its way through city centre streets at rush hour. It's using all the parts of its engine, no? The battery, the gasket, the drive shank . . . I'm not much of a mechanic, but you get the idea."

There was a small bubble of awkward laughter from about five students.

"But take that Porsche onto a motorway or freeway or whatever you Americans want to call it. Put your foot down. Push it to its top speed.

"It's still using the same engine parts as when crawling through rush hour, no? Only now, you're racing along at two hundred miles an hour. You are utilising the car's full potential.

"Now get rid of your standard, nasty fuel and pump it full of high-performance, high-grade petrol, and she's really purring.

"It is the same with the human brain. However much of it we might use every day, none of us uses it to its fullest potential. Supposedly, you can train it by playing Sudoku, solving crosswords, and avoiding alcohol. But, if you add some of that high-performance fuel, you have a chance of maximising its potential. And, when something gives the brain that sort of burst," he finished, staring into the young faces before him. "It is capable of achieving things that you can't even begin to imagine." . . .

. . . **MOIRA** Coe marched down the brightly lit corridor. Sunlight streamed through the windows, but Coe ignored the majestic beauty of the Finger Lakes region beyond them and focussed on her goal.

Students and staff swerved around her as though sensing the stranger's menace. However, they quickly continued about their business without giving her presence a second thought. It was one of her skills, one which would have saddened most people. But Moira Coe didn't have any problem with being forgettable. In fact, it was one of her greatest strengths.

Arriving at her destination, she rapped her knuckles on the office door. Silence greeted her.

Frustration bubbled inside her, but she fought it down, annoyed at herself for harbouring such a sensation, even for so short a time.

Hearing footsteps behind her, she whirled to see two young women hurrying by, books and folders clutched under their arms.

"You," she barked at them, flashing her forged Baltimore Police Department ID card. "Where can I find him?" she demanded.

The girls glanced at the name on the office door and then nodded down the corridor. "I think he's giving a lecture at the moment," one of the girls replied. "Hall 3, I think."

Coe nodded sternly, then brushed past the students towards Lecture Hall 3, on the hunt for Doctor Henri Moreau . . .

. . . **EMILY** Hamilton watched as the giant slave's eyelids fluttered open.

He lay on a bed in the servant's quarters at her father's estate outside of Port Royal. Convincing him to purchase the dying African from Charles Banks had not been easy, especially as the cowardly Banks had insisted on a small fortune in return. But she had persisted, highlighting that she owed the so-called Black Death her life. By the time the two men had relented, however, the Black Death, abandoned and ignored by his masters and fellow slaves alike, had been almost dead. The severe burns across his back, legs and arms were infected, and fever had taken hold.

Emily had barely left his side for three weeks now, much to her father's disgust. Rather, she sat by his bed, cleaning his wounds, bathing his burning forehead. She read to him, sang to him, confided in him. Yet never once had he opened his eyes.

Until now.

Emily knew she shouldn't have been surprised that his eyes did not wander about in confusion or fear. They were instantly alert, analysing his environment before locking onto her. Emily felt a shiver spread through her, relief mixed with unease.

"You . . . you saved me," she whispered. It was such a silly first thing to say to him, yet she could not stop herself. "Why?"

The intensity in his dark eyes burned more fiercely than the fire that had nearly claimed them both. His voice was barely audible when he replied, but his words froze Emily.

"I saw you fall before you did so," he said. "It was my destiny to save you . . ."

. . . **DRIZZLING** rain slanted across the harbourside. The sea-breeze propelled it with such force that it soaked Edward Pryce far more than the sprinkling of water alone could have done.

However, as he emerged from the horse-drawn carriage and laid eyes upon his new command, a three-masted, flat-bottomed bark, he spared no thought for the rain, the unseasonal frigidity or the featureless grey sky.

Readjusting his long, flowing black coat, he reached back into the carriage to retrieve his black tricorn, the golden gilding glinting in the muted sunlight. Seating it upon his head, he fetched his final belongings, marvelling once more at his new benefactor's ability to seemingly procure for him whatever he needed.

In this case, two items from his old cabin on the *L'aille Raptor*. Two items taken from the heathen who had exacted the curse of the Moon Mask upon him.

He swung his sword belt around his waist, then

sheaved his matching golden sword and dagger before heading towards his waiting ship.

And a meeting with destiny . . .

. . . **THE** ancient chamber exploded with multiple bursts of red light. Seven chemical light sticks splashed into the water, eliciting a panicked eruption of startled crocodiles. They thrashed about, angry at the second intrusion into their dark solitude in one day.

Nathan Raine slid silently through the hole in the chamber's ceiling, suspended on a high tensile metal cable. About halfway down, he slowed his descent, spinning in a lazy three-sixty. His eyes absorbed every detail, his mind translating that information into a 3D map in his minds-eye.

He let out a low whistle. "Sure is creepy down here," he said. Then, under his breath, he added. "I think Benny had the right idea about staying away."

Thinking about King conjured memories of Maria.

You must not go to the Dark Mountain, her voice sang once again in his head. A glimpse of inky blackness swallowing the land assaulted him, snippets of his Soul Flight returning to haunt him.

Raine hesitated, a chill creeping through him.

You must not go to the Dark Mountain.

Then, just as Nathan Raine always did, he pushed through his self-doubt and dropped the rest of the way into the chamber . . .

. . . **DARKNESS** blotted out the crisp blue sky.

It swept above Maria, plunging the clearing where she stood into shadow.

Just like in her Soul Flight.

Just like in her dreams, the nightmare she endured each night.

"A storm is coming."

Wakondi's baritone startled her. She looked up and realised the enormous swarm of bats that had scattered the villagers in a wave of panic had passed. They fled south, moving like a single miasmic entity.

"I know," Maria replied, her voice hushed, reverent. Her gaze turned towards the distant silhouette of Sarisariñama set against the azure sky. Rain clouds gathered below its summit, preparing to drop their daily torrent. Still, Maria knew Wakondi did not refer to the Amazon's daily rainstorm. Something else was gathering. There was no sign of it yet, but she felt its electric charge in the air, the scent of ozone teasing her nostrils, the muted calls of the jungle's wildlife sensing the coming danger.

But the upcoming weather system wasn't the only storm she sensed.

"A contact on the mountain tells me they've found a mask," she said. "The Face of *Cajushawa*. And now I sense that both halves of the Rain King are entering the Dark Mountain together." She nodded slowly, a picture of Nathan Raine and Benjamin King swirling in her minds-eye as though she was still submerged in the throes of a Soul Flight. "The prophecy is coming true." She sighed, a deep, weary sigh beyond her years.

"A storm is most certainly coming . . ."

To be continued in . . .

THE XIBALBA QUEST

JAMES RICHARDSON

A SMALL FAVOUR

I really hope you enjoyed this book and would like to read more of Raine and King's adventures.

Did you know that reviews not only help other readers choose their next literary delight but directly affect a book's visibility on a sales platform? Books with more positive reviews sell more and that lets budding authors like me write more and ultimately you, the reader, well, read more.

So, if you enjoyed this book, I'd really appreciate you submitting an honest review or rating (of course, if you didn't like it that's fine too, but please be kind).

I'd love to hear any direct feedback or comments so feel free to message me via email, social media or my website.

Thank you, James

@worldofmoonmask
james.richardson@moonmask.net
moonmask.net

THE SARISARINAMA EXPEDITION

Follow Dr Benjamin King's blog as he relates the trials and tribulations of the exciting Sarisariñama Expedition.
From an attempted kidnapping on the streets of Caracas to the perils of a journey through the jungle; from a terrifying plane crash to the dangers lying within the dark heart of the Labyrinth, experience the expedition in King's own words.

Turn the page for an exclusive extract

https://bit.ly/sarisarinamaexpedition

WWW.MOONMASK.NET

DAY 5

WE should have noticed that our taxicab wasn't one of the city's official while ones, and certainly not one of the hotel districts' black ones. But, hey, it was dark.

What started to ring the alarm bells in my head was how the driver spent a lot of time on his phone. My Spanish is good enough to know that he was updating someone about our journey.

We headed away from the Simon Bolivar International Airport, south down the Autopista Caracas, towards the main sprawl of the city.

Then, sure enough, we pulled off the main road into a seething labyrinth of motorbike-infested streets. We zigzagged through the maze, struggling to make out any details through the flickering orange of the occasional working street light. The boarded-up storefronts and graffiti-clad walls gave us little hope that we were in the touristic area of Altamira, where our pre-booked hotel was located.

Sid and I squeezed one another's hands in silence, confirming that we had both determined that something pretty serious was wrong.

A short while later, we pulled up outside a building with a flickering neon sign reading 'hotel'. Our driver insisted it was the Hotel Majestic, just as we had requested.

Dared we hope our concerns were for nothing and that Altamira was just a bit crappy?

A most accommodating hotel staff member appeared and rushed to open our door. They were fully booked, he advised us. Fortunately, they had a sister hotel just a few minutes down the road that the taxi would happily take us to.

If something smelt fishy before, now it smelt like a fishmonger's had exploded.

This was a scam, and Sid and I knew it.

The Hotel Majestic was nowhere in sight, but we sure as hell weren't going to get sucked into this pair's money-making scheme.

In hindsight, we should have counted our blessings. In a city regularly labelled the 'Murder Capital of the World', our run-in with crime was nothing more than a 'hotel swap scam'. Gap Year students fall for them every day. Indeed, my dad and I had a similar experience in Hanoi years ago.

Instead, indignant at the audacity of the attempted scam, I flung open the car door as the hotel assistant was about to close it again. Sid followed me out, as did, moments later, the equally indignant driver. We wrenched our bags from the boot and hauled them onto our backs, ignoring a tirade of angry exchanges.

The driver, realising his fiendish scheme had backfired and we would not be staying at his friend's nearby hotel, demanded we pay $40 for the taxi fare.

After initially refusing, I sensed some increasing threat from the man, so I threw him a $10 note, per our initial negotiation. More than generous, considering a journey from the airport to our desired hotel should have been $3, and we were nowhere near said desired hotel.

That wasn't enough for him.

We walked away, eyeing the dodgy looking backstreet warily. But we were committed now. Committed to navigating this place, in the dark, with no idea of where we were or how to get to where we needed to be. The driver followed, becoming angrier and angrier, demanding more money. No taxis were in sight, no prominent public places like restaurants or cafes to seek aid in, and no sign of police. There were only bikes zipping down the street, the angry growl of their engines bouncing from the walls. The few shady characters darting and flitting through the shadows like wraiths ignored our plight.

And that's when I heard the last thing you want to hear your girlfriend cry out in the middle of the murder capital of the world.

"He's got a gun!"